S. Baring Gould

The Icelander's sword or the story of Oraefadal by S. Baring-Gould

S. Baring Gould

The Icelander's sword or the story of Oraefadal by S. Baring-Gould

ISBN/EAN: 9783743333109

Manufactured in Europe, USA, Canada, Australia, Japa

Cover: Foto ©Andreas Hilbeck / pixelio.de

Manufactured and distributed by brebook publishing software
(www.brebook.com)

S. Baring Gould

The Icelander's sword or the story of Oraefadal by S. Baring-Gould

THE AURORA FLASHED CRIMSON—DOWN CAME THORARIN'S WEAPON, SWEEPING
ERIC'S SWORD ASIDE WITH ONE MIGHTY BLOW.

THE

ICELANDER'S SWORD

OR

The Story of Oraefa=dal

BY

S. BARING GOULD

AUTHOR OF

'MEHALAH,' 'GRETTIR THE STRONG,' ETC.

Methuen & Co.

18, BURY STREET, LONDON, W.C.

1894

INTRODUCTION

THIS little story was written for boys in 1858, and I believe it interested them. Since then, in 1861, I visited Iceland. I have been able to correct some inaccuracies into which I had fallen through lack of personal acquaintance with the country. Boys are the same ever, and what pleased boys thirty-six years ago may perhaps please boys of the new generation.

CONTENTS

CONTENTS

THE ICELANDER'S SWORD;

OR

THE STORY OF ORÆFA-DAL

CHAPTER I.

A NORWEGIAN FOREST.

WILD night in Norway; the moon had just been clouded over by piles of gray mist, which rolled through the sky, sending out arms of vapour; and, haggard and ghastly, she seemed to steal over her course, swathed in corpse-clothes. Now and then some crags caught a straggling gleam and flashed forth, but directly after were again blotted out; while far below, a frozen fiord was shining like steel, till the shadow turned it to lead. An uncertain light flickered down the mountain-side and over

Fighting the wolves

1

the pine-forests, which raved and bent as the wind poured through them.

Occasionally, as the storm lulled, the low howl of the wolf rendered the night more dreary still to a lad who had lost his way, and was standing on a cliff which rose abruptly from an icebound tarn. The youth looked around for some light to guide his steps, but in vain; and then, with a despairing sigh, he plunged at random into the forest. The larches clashed overhead; at times the wind rent them apart, and showed him the sky in a gray gash; at others, it heaped the branches together before him like a black wave. His feet struck against the roots, or stumbled over stones, till, weary and hopeless of finding his way, he paused, and leaned against the bole of a large fir.

'This is strange!' thought he. 'I know there is a shed where I can rest the night somewhere near here; I shall be frozen if I remain out.'

After some moments he pushed on again. Occasionally, where the trees were more straggling, he had thick drifts of snow to toil through; the descent was no longer precipitous, and the scattered rocks diminished in number. Suddenly the lad stopped, as a faint shout from the distance came down with the wind. Before Magnus (that was the boy's name) lay a patch of snow covering a small glade in the forest. The moon broke from among the clouds, and, as it lit up the open ground, showed him a wolf moving among the firs at the further end, and stealing out from the snow; he saw it stand for a moment still, utter a low howl, and then trot slowly across the snow-field without noticing him.

Before Magnus had moved from where he had been standing, the shout was repeated, accompanied by the howlings of several wolves, fierce, but still distant. A chill ran through the boy's limbs, and the fear of spending a night among these animals, rendered savage with hunger, gave him strength to push on. At the same time a wave of mist ran over the moon, and obscured it.

He fell frequently; at times his foot sank between rocks, the crevices of which had been filled and smoothed over with snow; at others, he ran against some bough, which in the thick darkness he had not seen. The howls of the wolves seemed nearer, and were answered by others on all sides.

'I can go no further,' groaned Magnus, falling exhausted on a drift: 'if these brutes come to tear me to pieces, I can escape by climbing a fir;' then, after a pause, he said, 'Perhaps I had better search for a convenient tree now, while I have the time.'

Out from among the driving clouds again streamed a passing gush of moonlight. Magnus gave a cry of joy; the snow heap on which he had fallen was piled against the side of the log barn of which he had been in search. He looked in, but all was so obscure that he could only grope his way along; the door itself had fallen, and the snow was heaped over it on the threshold. After having gone round the shed, feeling with his hands, Magnus found that there was a loft about five feet from the ground, in which, probably, hay had been kept; to this he managed to climb, by mounting on a broken manger. The floor was gone in many places, but sufficient remained for him to lie upon.

No sooner had he settled himself, however, than the recollection of the other wanderer in the forest forced itself upon him, and springing down, he went to the door.

Just then the calls were redoubled, and this time close at hand; a man's powerful voice was shouting for help. Magnus called in reply as loudly as he could; and, from the yelping which approached, he felt certain that there was a troop of wolves following, if not yet attacking the man. Accordingly he did his utmost to clear the snow from the door, and to lift it; but he had not time to place it in the opening before he saw what appeared at first to be a moving shadow among the trees. As it came out on the snow he distinguished a man, with a child on his left arm, surrounded by a pack of wolves, which he succeeded in keeping at a distance with his great Norwegian sword, brandished in his right hand. At times the wolves retreated behind him, then a few would dash ahead growling, and, as he came near the barn, they seemed to comprehend that a place of refuge was accessible, and rushed about him like a wave, pouring in at the door, driving Magnus from it, and obliging him to escape to the loft.

The traveller entered the doorway with difficulty, or the wolves were striving to spring upon him from behind.

'Here, here!' shouted the boy. 'Come to me— here is a loft here. Give me your hand; I will help you up.'

' Take this child first,' said the man, as he lifted it towards the place whence he heard the voice proceed. The boy's eyes were accustomed to the darkness, and he could discern sufficiently to lift the child and place it in safety.

' Offspring of Loki!' exclaimed the man, as at the moment a couple of wolves sprang upon him. Magnus felt about for a piece of wood, and snatching up a broken plank, leaped into the midst of the shed. Having a large knife with him, he drew it from his girdle, and drove it into the throat of one of the beasts which had fastened upon the traveller. Then, seeing that the man had succeeded in throwing off the other, Magnus laid about him vigorously with his weapon, till, as he thought, he had driven the wolves from the shed, his companion at the same time sweeping his sword right and left.

' Help me with this!' exclaimed the lad, flinging down his piece of wood, grasping the door with both hands, and swinging it into its place. ' Bring something to put against it,' he added hurriedly; but hearing a violent struggle behind him, he turned and leaned his own back against it; the darkness within was now so complete that he could see nothing, but he heard the man dashing to and fro, and the snarling breath of a wolf at his throat.

Magnus dared not leave the door, against which the wolves were leaping from without; but he held his knife in readiness to plunge into the brute the moment he had an opportunity.

The struggling became more and more violent; now and then the man and wolf crashed against the walls of the shed, and finally fell, rolling and plunging on the floor. Magnus bent forward, and, putting forth his hand, felt the shaggy coat of the beast; instantly he drove his knife in as far as the hilt would allow.

The wolf lifted its head, uttered a fierce growl, and flew at the man's throat again.

A death struggle ensued; the combatants rose and fell one over the other. In his agony of desire to render some assistance, the boy for a moment ventured to leave the door; but the pack without continued dashing at it, endeavouring to force it open, and he was compelled to throw himself against it once more.

At the same time, by a desperate effort the stranger raised himself to his feet, shook the beast furiously, but ineffectually, and then fell against the door with such violence that the whole building shivered, and a portion of the old and decayed roof fell heavily in; a beam dropped close by Magnus, but without touching him, and he had the presence of mind to lift and fix it against the door, so as to bar it thoroughly. Through the gap in the roof a ray of moonlight struggled in, showing the gray wolf lying dead upon the fallen man, its blood mingled with his.

The boy stooped and looked at the traveller, who was alive, but had his breast and shoulder horribly mangled, and his throat nearly torn away, so that his breath came with a whistle through the ragged gashes of his windpipe, making and bursting great bubbles of blood. With a feeble motion the dying man pointed towards the child, which was sobbing

bitterly in the loft; he tried to speak, but his words
died away in a rattle and splutter; this was his last
effort; the face grew rapidly grayer and colder as the
blood gushed from a torn artery in the neck, forming
a dark pool in the trampled snow; and in a few
moments the eye became fixed and glassy.

Magnus climbed to the loft, and taking the child in
his arms, wrapped it in the cloak which he had previously spread on the boards, and endeavoured to
lull it to sleep.

That was a dreadful night; the wolves tried repeatedly to get in at the door, and some of them even
scrambled up the snow-drift, and looked in through the
hole in the broken roof. After a time the moon set,
and at length, wearied with their ineffectual attempts,
the pack slunk away, and dispersed, though their continuous howling drove all thought of sleep from the
besieged youth. When, at length, morning dawned,
Magnus descended from his place of safety, to open
the door and let in additional light.

In order to effect this, he had to move the two
bodies, and clear away some of the rubbish that had
fallen from above. On admitting the light a ghastly
sight presented itself to him. The man was apparently of middle age, his features hard and
weather-beaten. His dress showed him to be an
Icelander; the trousers were of sealskin; the cloak,
which was trodden and stained, had been handsome,
and was of purple, lined with white fur; the sword,
moreover, gave signs of the possessor having belonged to no humble class, as it was of foreign workmanship.

The blood had frozen on the ground, and hung in clots of red ice to the grizzled coat of the wolf.

Magnus considered for some time before he decided how to act; at length he picked up the sword and dug a hole in the snow-drift large enough to serve as a temporary grave; and into this he lifted the corpse and piled snow over it; then, slinging the sword across his back, he returned to the child, and having gently lifted it down, carried it out in his arms, thinking it best to remove it, while still sleeping, from the scene of last night's horrors.

Magnus could now examine his burden; he saw that it was a boy of about seven years old, and that his face was colourless and pinched with cold.

'It is a pity that I do not know the father's name,' thought he.

· 'Where's father?' asked the little fellow, opening his eyes.

'I cannot tell you now,' answered Magnus. 'Can you walk?'

'Yes, put me down; but where is my father?'

'You cannot see him now,' replied the elder boy; 'now, tell me, what is your name?'

'Asmund,' replied the boy.

'And your father's?'

'Why, *father*,' was the answer, as the child stared up into Magnus's face, as if astonished at the question.

CHAPTER II.

HO does not know the pleasure of returning to a warm fireside after a long journey in the cold? Ah, reader! you can guess better than I can describe the feelings of Magnus in the evening, as he led his companion into the wooden hall of Thordsa Farm.

'Well, Magnus,' exclaimed his father, Gregorius, 'you have returned safely at last; but whom have you brought with you?'

'An orphan,' replied the boy. 'His father was killed by wolves last night in the forest; we must go to-morrow morning and bury him. I have covered him with snow, but there is a thaw setting in.'

'And what is to be done with the child?' asked Gregorius.

'There is no knowing who his father may have been,' said Magnus. 'But as he is here, here he must remain.'

Gregorius nodded his head, and so the matter was settled.

The hall was large and lofty, formed entirely of wood; in the centre of the area a large fire of pine-logs sent its smoke up a funnel, like that we see nowadays over a blacksmith's forge. About the walls were hung bearskins, horns, and weapons; among them shone conspicuously Gregorius' blue shield, spangled with gold stars, and his mighty sword Hneitir. The bonder himself, his brother Rolf and daughter Ingibjorg, were at the fire, and, as but little light penetrated into the room through the small round windows, over which parchment was drawn, especially now that it was dusky without, the red flicker fell full on the figures of those seated round the hearth.

Gregorius was an elderly man, his hair already turning gray, his countenance noble and open, and a calm intelligence sparkled in his honest blue eyes. Rolf was somewhat younger, and though apparently lacking the talent of his brother, his features were homely and pleasing. Ingibjorg was little more than a girl, with a beautiful and rather pale face; her rich brown hair was knotted back under a quaint head-dress, from beneath which, in places, it strayed in shining locks.

'Ingibjorg, where is Thorarin?' asked Magnus.

'Hunting,' replied his sister. 'He is gone with Erling Skialgson's party.'

'He will return hungry,' said Gregorius; 'and, at all events, Magnus and the child must want something. Come, Ingibjorg, get some food ready for them.'

The girl slowly rose, and went in search of a servant.

'I believe that I have got this firm at last,' said Rolf, who had been fitting an axe-head to the haft. 'I shall go down and have a look over the *Dragon* to-morrow, brother; you have not put to sea in her for a long while. Ulf came to me to-day to say that some planks needed repairing; they must be put to rights soon. The ship is likely to be wanted now the spring is setting in.'

'True,' answered Gregorius thoughtfully; 'the king will be summoning a Thing* before long, I am sure, and there is certain to be fighting in the coming summer, so King Magnus will require his lendermen to be ready with assistance.'

'The old *Dragon* is seaworthy enough still,' observed Rolf; 'she is a fine ship. This winter's ice may, however, have injured her a little.'

'Not much,' replied Gregorius. 'See to the head being painted afresh, Rolf.'

'Ay, I will,' said the other; 'and I have been thinking that a great gilt spike on the *Dragon's* nose would improve the appearance.'

Asmund had been sitting quietly, warming himself, and smiling with pleasure at the red flames,

* A 'Thing' was an assembly of bonders.

while Magnus sang abstractedly to himself in a low tone :

> ' Quake, old wolf, in your firm chain,
> Mitgard's serpent writhe in pain,
> Baldur comes in light again.'

' Tell me all about the wolf Fenrir,' said Asmund, turning suddenly round, and interrupting him ; ' I know you can tell me the story, and I am never tired of it.'

' I can,' said Magnus ; ' but, you know, it is all nonsense to a Christian child.'

' Yes, yes,' exclaimed the little boy vehemently, ' as if stones had roots and women beards !'

' Well,' began the elder, smiling, ' Loki, the evil god, had a son called Fenrir, and this son was a wolf.'

' Yes,' interrupted Asmund. ' It was quite a little thing once, but it grew and grew, and got so large— but go on fast.'

' Well, then,' continued Magnus, ' the gods were afraid of Fenrir—he was so grim and fierce, his horrid gray sides were ever panting, as if he were thirsting for their blood. So they wrought a chain to bind him with called Læding, and they asked the wolf to suffer them to tie him in it, just to see whether he were able to break it.'

' He did,' cried Asmund gleefully. ' Go on to the women's beards.'

' You are interrupting my story,' said Magnus ; ' that will not do. The chain was put about the wolf, and he stretched himself and it snapped immediately.'

'I know it did,' said Asmund. 'Go on.'

'Then the gods made a still stronger chain, called Dromi, and they bade Fenrir try this one about him. He looked at it, and knowing that his strength had increased since he burst Læding, allowed him-self to be fastened with it ; then shaking himself, he heaved his gray sides, and rolled on the ground. The fetter burst at once, link from link.'

'Now go on to Gleipnir,' said Asmund, his eyes sparkling in the firelight with pleasure.

'So the gods sent to the home of the Black Elves to have a third chain fashioned. These little folk formed it of six things—the sound of a cat's foot-fall, the beards of women, the roots of stones, the sinews of bears, the breath of fish, and the spittle of birds.' Here the child broke into a joyous laugh, and clapped his hands. 'This chain,' continued Magnus, 'was no thicker than a piece of silk thread, yet Fenrir was loath to have it wound about him, for he dreaded treachery; and the gods tried in vain to persuade him, till finally he consented, on condition of one of them putting his hand into his mouth, as a pledge that no deceit was meditated.'

'I think,' said the child meditatively, 'that the gods did not behave quite honourably and fairly by Fenrir. They should have told him openly what they intended. They were many, and he was one.'

'I agree with you,' said Magnus ; 'but we Christian boys have higher thoughts than heathen gods. But to continue. The gods looked at one another wistfully, uncertain what to do ; but Tyr stepped forth, and thrust his hand between the wolf's huge jaws.'

' Tyr was brave,' said Asmund.

' Yes, very,' replied the other. ' Then, when Fenrir was fast chained, he tried to burst the fetter, but in vain ; and the gods all laughed aloud, all but Tyr, whose hand the wolf bit off. The gods then took the end of the chain, and drew it through the middle of a rock, which they sank deep in the earth ; and as the wolf opened his jaws to bite at them, they ran a sword through his mouth, which pierced the under jaw as far as the hilt, so that the point touched the palate.'

' And the foam—tell me about that,' said the child.

' Well, then, the foam from the brute's mouth, flowing continually, makes the great frothing river Von.'

The story was scarce ended when the door was dashed open, and a young man walked in, accompanied by a couple of dogs much of the nature of wolves. His wild dark eyes wandered about the hall ; coming up to the fire, he stood there rattling his weapons.

' Look here, Ingibjorg,' said he, drawing from off his back a couple of wolf-skins, the paws of which he had fastened over his breast, and flinging them down, ' I am going to make leggings out of these creatures' skins. Oh, I brought the old one down like this !' and poising his spear, he hurled it across the hall.

' I have hit it !' cried he, with a shout of laughter ' by Loki and the holy Olaf I have !'

'Thorarin, my son,' exclaimed Gregorius, 'be more discreet in your vows. Swear not by our blessed saint and the devil Loki together.'

'Well, by anything you like, father,' said the young man, still laughing. 'Look, I have hit it!'

'What have you hit?' asked Ingibjorg.

'Why, I have broached it—the butt of mead.'

'Senseless boy!' exclaimed Gregorius, leaping angrily from his seat.

'Oh, father,' cried Thorarin, snatching Ingibjorg's head-dress off, 'the leak is soon mended;' and striding across the hall, he snapped the spear-shaft which had entered the butt short off, rammed the head-dress in with the end of the spear, and then left it sticking out of the vessel. 'There, sister,' shouted he, laughing, 'that is all your woman's head-gear is fit for—to bung a broached beer-butt with.' Ingibjorg began an angry retort, but her brother cut her short. 'Ah, you silly girl, you do not know how pretty you are now, with all your hair over your shoulders. These caps suit you badly.'

'Well, Thorarin,' said she, somewhat appeased, 'you have quite spoiled it, and you must give me something instead.'

'I will, by the Valkyri,' swore the youth. 'Anything—a live wolf, if you like, or a bear and its cubs.'

Gregorius still looked vexed; Rolf continued stolidly mending a hatchet. Asmund gazed with wondering eyes into the young man's face.

'Well, Thorarin,' cried Ingibjorg sharply, 'what are you doing now?'

Her brother was kicking his savage wolf-dogs to and fro towards the fire.

'These are my own dogs,' said the huntsman good-humouredly. 'Now, then, Schlurker, you hound! will you go back?' and he kicked the brute violently on the head.

'Thorarin!' expostulated his sister, in an angry tone of voice. 'You are driving the animal into the fire.'

'Well, to be sure, little sister,' answered the youth, 'I only want to make it singe its tail, and get it angry, then we shall have a merry game together.'

Thereupon he dealt a blow at the dog with his remaining spear. The animal snarled, and showed its fangs; Thorarin kicked it back on the live embers, and Schlurker, with a yell of pain, flew at him.

'Now, come on, dear friend,' shouted its master joyously, seizing it, and flinging it from him. The brute was at him again, but he caught it, and after a struggle, which elicited peals of laughter from his merry breast, he gagged it, holding his spear crossways in its mouth.

'Are you going to be quiet at last?' asked his sister; 'for if you are, I will have supper brought in.'

'I am only playing,' apologized Thorarin. 'Now you come and have a romp with the dog. I will take the spear from its mouth.'

'No, no,' exclaimed Ingibjorg, hurrying out of the hall.

Till the supper was ready the light-hearted youth

amused himself with pacifying his dog ; and he and it came to ready and amicable terms when, having snatched a piece of meat from a platter just brought in, he threw it to the dogs.

' Thorarin !' almost shrieked his sister, ' you have thrown all the joint to those creatures. Now you must satisfy yourself on the curds.'

' It is your fault,' said the huntsman, laughing. ' Why did you not have enough roasted for father, the dogs, Uncle Rolf, and me—for us all ?'

' You are a thorough heathen,' said Ingibjorg indignantly.

' Ay, little sister, that I am, in Lent, but not at Yule.'

Thorarin having flung all the meat away, there remained for consumption only a dish of curds, and another of flour and milk, flavoured with whortleberries, which had been preserved with honey in jars.

' Brother,' said Rolf, during the meal, ' I suppose that you have heard the message neighbour Hlenni has sent. His man came here while you were out, but you must have heard it.'

' Indeed I have not,' answered Gregorius. ' What was it ?'

' He complains that some of our men who have been over his land have carried off a score of his sheep, and have set fire to a barn.'

' Have they ?' asked the bonder. ' If so, let sheep for sheep be returned.'

' I do not believe a word of it,' answered Rolf. ' I have questioned our men, and they stoutly deny it.'

2

'It is a lie of Hlenni!' broke in Thorarin. 'I met the rascal to-day, and had a little talk with him.'

'Have you quarrelled?' asked Gregorius angrily. 'Thorarin, you are continually getting me into trouble with my neighbours through your violence, and let me tell you it is a far harder matter to get out of a scrape than to get into one. Any fool can do the latter, but it takes a wise man to do the former.'

'I did not quarrel with him, but whether he has quarrelled with me is another thing. The fellow charged me with the loss of his sheep, and I offered to fight it out with him, just in a friendly way; it would settle the business so quickly. He walked aside, so I drew my sword, and whirled it about his face. Oh, father! to see his expression of fright, and the way he winked his eyes.'

The young man leaned back in his seat laughing. Gregorius' brow clouded over.

'When you have done laughing——' he began, but Thorarin interrupted him.

'Father, do not blame me. I made some verses about him, which I sang, and my men and some of his began to titter. I promise you he looked as black as a thunderstorm.'

The bonder, fully irritated, turned towards his son, and said:

'I tell you this, Thorarin, your own deeds be on your own head. I shall take up none of your quarrels for you; fight them out, or not, just as you like.'

' Fight !' exclaimed the young Norwegian; ' as if I would not give my best spear, or even old Schlurker, to have a sword fight with Hlenni any day in the week excepting Sunday.'

' It may be pleasure to you to get into broils,' retorted Gregorius; ' but, my son, it is no pleasing prospect for me to look forward to barns set fire to and cattle killed.'

' Let Hlenni dare to do such a thing,' said Thorarin vehemently, ' and I will go and burn him in his house if I can catch him ; if not, burn his house and goods, whether you help me or not.'

' Now then, Thorarin,' expostulated Ingibjorg, ' you had better stop talking and boasting that you can do mischief.'

CHAPTER III.

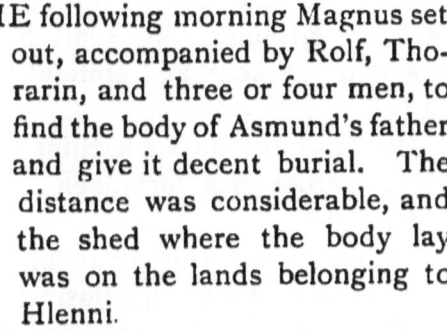

THE following morning Magnus set out, accompanied by Rolf, Thorarin, and three or four men, to find the body of Asmund's father and give it decent burial. The distance was considerable, and the shed where the body lay was on the lands belonging to Hlenni.

Magnus wore the magnificent sword of the dead man, slung across his back; every now and then Thorarin would admire it, and drawing it from his brother, would whirl it round his head and lop off a pine bough. Magnus, too, had further opportunity now for observing it, and he could not but admire its beauty, the temper of the steel, and the richly enamelled hilt.

On reaching the shed they found Hlenni, with several others, already there.

Thorarin could not restrain his delight. 'Magnus,' said he gleefully, 'we shall have sport to-day in worrying the sour and spiteful bonder, coward that he is!'

'Better have no such thing,' said Rolf bluntly. 'Your father has forbidden it; why should we quarrel?'

Hlenni, seeing the advancing party, approached, and asked Rolf what his business was there.

'Business, man!' exclaimed the latter. 'Why, a good Christian work of mercy—the burial of the dead.'

'We are before you,' observed the bonder, scowling round on the group. 'How knew you anything about a dead man being here?'

'I was with him when he died; the wolves tore him,' said Magnus.

'Ay,' answered Hlenni, 'the marks in the snow and the blood have told me that wolves have been here; but where is the child?'

'How know you anything about the man and his child?'

'He came to my farm, and pushed on his way after having stayed awhile with me; you have his sword!'

'Wherefore not?' asked Magnus sharply.

'It is mine,' answered the bonder, putting out his hand to grasp it. 'The man died on my property; mean you to steal his sword!'

'Steal it!' retorted Magnus, his eye kindling.

' I have as good a right to it as you, and a better ;
I was with him when he died, and I have the care of
his child.'

'The sword is mine by rights,' said Hlenni violently.
' Give it me.'

'What need have you of the sword,' asked
Thorarin—'you who wink and wince at the sight
of one? Magnus, if you give it him, wrap it in wool,
or he will not dare to touch it.'

'I have no thought of letting him have it,' said
Magnus. 'The sword is my own.'

'Fight it out with me,' exclaimed Thorarin, leaping forward and lifting his sword. 'Now, Hlenni, show
that you are a man, or I will send you a present of a
pair of petticoats.'

'Draw sword on you !' cried the bonder contemptuously ; 'I never fight with boys.'

'I am no lad,' said Rolf, stepping forward. 'Speak
with me. This sword leaves not its present owner ;
let things be. You have got the dead man's cloak,
I see——'

'Ay, but trampled on and torn !' answered
Hlenni.

'It is soiled,' said Rolf; 'it is not torn. It is of
some value ; keep that, and let no more be said about
the sword. Magnus has saved the stranger's child ;
it is but right that he should keep what he has got, as
some recompense for what he has done.'

'It is mine by rights,' persisted Hlenni.

'Will you fight me ?' shouted Thorarin, pushing his
uncle aside. 'Draw your sword at once, coward, or
by the Valkyri I'll send you a distaff.'

' I am in no humour to pay mulct for your death,'
said Hlenni sulkily.

' Pay mulct !' cried the young man with a laugh.
' You have not killed me yet ; if I pay mulct for you,
it will be but the price of an old woman's murder, so
I am content to fight.'

' Thorarin, be silent,' said Rolf. ' Hlenni, let
matters rest as they are.'

The bonder stood scowling at them all for a
moment, and then, turning on his heel, said, ' I
shall cite you before the next Thing and claim the
sword.'

' And you will not get it,' rejoined Thorarin.

' Stop !' exclaimed Magnus, hastening after the
bonder, and catching him by the sleeve. ' Tell me
the name of the man who has been killed by wolves,
and you shall have the sword.'

Hlenni turned round and looked at him ; his
lips moved ; then he compressed them and fixed his
eye on Magnus coldly. ' Do you not know ?' he asked.

' No,' answered the boy, ' or I should not have
asked you.'

' Nor do I know,' answered the bonder. ' He was
a stranger to me when he stopped at Guttorm's-dal,
I never asked his name;' and turning again, he
rejoined his men, who had in the meanwhile removed the body, and dug a grave sufficiently deep to
receive it.

Rolf and his party retreated, leaving Hlenni to
finish the work on which he was engaged.

' Thorkel,' said Hlenni, ' why did you not tell me
of this man's death before ?'

' I did not see the body till this morning,' answered
the churl. 'I was passing this way, and, seeing the
ground trampled and bloody, I looked in at the shed
door. The wolves had begun to tear up the snow
where the body lay; and, besides, one end of the
cloak appeared from the drift. I could not have told
you of it before.'

' Do you know the name of the stranger ?'

' No,' replied Thorkel. ' All I know of him is that
he stopped a day at your farm, and that he had a child
with him, which I suppose the wolves must have torn
to pieces.'

When speaking with Magnus, Hlenni had been
beyond ear-shot of his men; accordingly he answered
that he supposed it was so.

' What was his name?' asked Thorkel. ' That cloak
belonged to no mean person.'

The bonder shook his head.

' I know not,' said he. ' Come, if you have finished
your work, give me the cloak; the weather is cold,
and we will return to pass a bowl of mead round, at
Guttorm's-dal.'

Hlenni walked on silently.

' I shall be revenged,' said he to himself, ' and that
without risking anything myself; other hands can
do the business for me. I have no mind to have
that firebrand Thorarin about my house and barns,
setting them in a blaze; no, I must have my revenge
without compromising myself. Thorkel !' said he ·
aloud, at the same time turning round, ' I may want
to send you to Iceland this spring; the snows and
frosts will be soon breaking up; you will have to go

to Viken—Sigurd Selson sails thence, and he will take you along with him.   I shall want you to carry a letter for me to my friend, the Lady Gudruna of Hraunvellir ; I shall be going about the same time to a Thing.'

CHAPTER IV.

THE ENEMY IN THE FIORD.

Rolf hauling Erling.

HE spring advanced rapidly. The waters of the fiord, freed from their ice, quivered on the shingle; a cloud of green appeared to swim over the shores, as the feathery birch burst into leaf, and the larch covered itself with its bright green hair, which contrasted strongly with the sombre masses of pine higher up the slopes. Here and there a stream gushed down from some crag, or flowed unseen through a dense coppice. As the days lengthened, and as the air became daily more balmy, boats from the bonders' houses were frequently to be seen dropping down the fiord, as farm-servants went out fishing, or parties visited neighbouring homesteads. The *Dragon* floated at anchor near Gregorius' farm; the head had been re-gilded, and the ship put into thorough repair.

One fresh morning Rolf and Gregorius went on board, in order to examine her; and after having gone over the whole vessel, Rolf observed:

'You see, brother, it is as well to be prepared in case of danger. I hear that King Harald is about with a fleet; he was up the Folga Fiord last week, and they say that he is coming here soon; for the matter of that, he may be at the head of the fiord already, in which case we may suffer, although we have not as yet shown whom we favour.'

'I wonder much which side Hlenni will take in these troubles,' said Gregorius. 'I observed his boat passing Thordsoe this morning; the party were rowing swiftly, and Hlenni himself was in the stern.'

'There is mischief afloat,' answered Rolf. 'I know that Hlenni is on the side of King Harald; at least, that is what his people say; our folk have had some strife with them on the subject.'

'Then, for what purpose can he be going down the fiord?' asked Gregorius. 'He can have no particular business that way.'

'Here,' exclaimed Rolf, 'I'll hail that boat as it approaches, and ask if Erling has seen Hlenni pass; that is Erling's boat, and it seems that he is making towards our homestead.'

Directly Rolf called, the rowers paused on their oars and directed the boat towards the *Dragon*.

'Why, Erling himself is on board!' said Gregorius. 'It seems as if all the bonders were on the water to-day.'

In a few moments, the skiff was alongside of the ships; in another moment Erling had leaped on deck.

'I was bound for your farm,' said he. 'There is no time to be lost; something must be done. Harald is in the waters at the mouth of the fiord, and will drop down soon. He has burned the Folga Farm. I believe that most of the bonders are on his side, so he will do little till he comes towards our end.'

'You may depend, brother,' broke in Rolf, 'he will be down here at latest to-morrow. How many ships has he?'

'I cannot tell,' replied Erling. 'He has left some at the mouth of the inlet; however, I believe there are only three with him now.'

'Did you mark Hlenni's boat pass down a while ago?' asked Gregorius.

'Yes,' answered Skialgson; 'it was rowed down the fiord, and is going to Harald, I have no doubt.'

'Who, then, are there to meet the king?' asked Gregorius; 'except yourself and my people, there are none on the side of King Magnus, and we can look for no help.'

'None,' said the neighbour positively; 'except at the Folga Farm, all are for Harald Gille.'

'What is to be done?' exclaimed Rolf. 'We

cannot resist, or we shall be cut to pieces, and all our houses burned.'

'There can be no doubt about that,' said Gregorius thoughtfully. 'It is in vain to think of such a thing as resistance; what do you purpose doing, neighbour?'

'I shall escape to the woods as fast as I can,' Erling replied; 'I shall have time to move most of my stock, and Harald is not likely to remain here long; he has enough on his hands.'

'I hardly know what to decide on,' said Gregorius, 'whether to hide in the woods, or to trust to the *Dragon*, and drop behind Thordsoe into one of the little coves; the vessel would be perfectly concealed, and the enemy would in all probability suppose that we had fled to the mountains.'

'Trust to the sea rather than to the land,' advised Rolf; 'that is the true Norseman's creed.'

'I should recommend that course,' said Erling. 'If we both take refuge in the forest, the enemy will be more likely to find one or other of us, as together we should make a large body to conceal.'

'Then I'll trust to the *Dragon*, neighbour; thanks to you for having come to warn me in time. I must make haste to get my effects on board, or hidden.'

'My goods are being removed now,' said Erling. 'By to-night Erlingsdal will be deserted. Fare you well, till this trouble is over. By the way, in case you are in great need of help, let there be some signal between us.' Erling looked round; at last he said: 'There is a dead pine on the Skald's rock, round the next bend of the fiord; my place of refuge

will be within sight of that, or at all events I shall
have someone stationed to watch it.   If you want
assistance, set fire to the tree, and I will come down
on your farm with all my men, as I shall be hidden
close by Thordsâ-sund.'   So saying, with a shake
of the hand, the worthy bonder swung himself over
the side into his boat, and rowed briskly towards his
own farm.

No sooner had the news of danger spread than a
scene of bustle ensued at the farm.   Gregorius and
Rolf were engaged in giving directions during the
remainder of the day as to where some valuables
were to be hidden, and what others were to be
removed.   The cattle were driven to a sœter* on the
mountains, accompanied by most of the maidens and
some of the farm servants, carrying with them all
the dairy utensils.   Magnus was sent in a boat down
the fiord to watch for Hlenni, whom Rolf and his
brother wished to keep in ignorance of their projected
escape; so that, should he be returning, Magnus
might give notice in time to enable them to desist
from embarkation, and, if possible, to get the ship
into deep water off shore, before he came in sight
of it.

Gregorius did not feel any great anxiety on the
subject himself, however, for he considered it more
than probable that Hlenni would remain with King
Harald till the ships sailed up the fiord; and his
conjecture proved to be right, for there was no sign
of the boat's return, till, all being safe, and the house
completely gutted, Gregorius and those who were to

* A dairy-farm.

go on shipboard with him heaved up the anchor, after having signalled to and received Magnus, who reported that all was tranquil further down. Then the *Dragon* slowly rolled with the tide into the deep water, and was rowed steadily down towards Thordsoe.

Before proceeding, it will be necessary to give a slight sketch of the scene.

A Norwegian fiord often extends for many miles inland; the hills on each side fold one upon another, so that the water is broken into beautiful sheets like lakes, at times extending in long reaches, with a birch and pine covered belt of hills to all appearance closing it; but when the boat has approached the extremity, the rocks open, and a fresh expanse of sparkling water lies before the rower, winding off in another direction, and again apparently land-locked. Here and there an islet starts up, rugged and tufted with birch, or else, when nearer the mouth of the fiord, white with the feathers and traces of the sea-fowl. Here and there also the fiord will be broken up into lesser inlets, which dive behind hills and rocks, so that no conception of their extent can be formed, unless they be severally explored.

Thordsoe was a beautiful islet at the mouth of one of these creeks. The main waters of the estuary swept past Gregorius' farm of Thordsâ-sund, and veering to the left, and turning a headland covered with heather, after a reach of five or six miles, washed the sands by the boat-house of Guttorm's-dal, near Hlenni's house.

The basin before Thordsâ-sund was of but small

extent; out of it, however, on the right opened the creek blocked by Thordsoe. This little inlet was almost concealed by the island, which shot with a perpendicular scarp from the sea-level on one side, but shelved gently, covered with coppice, towards the water on that nearer the house, leaving a channel too shallow to be traversed by any vessel of burden, while on the abrupt flank it sank to a great depth. Almost directly, the creek doubled the spur of a hill, and was frittered into several smaller inlets which, though narrow, were of such depth that a ship could float in them at ease. The earth seemed to have undergone some great internal convulsion, which had rent its surface so as to form deep gashes, into which the sea had flowed, forming a labyrinth of small harbours. Gregörius knew well enough that the enemy could not pursue him into these recesses with their ships, as navigation there was dangerous to all but those who knew the soundings thoroughly ; and pursuit by land was hardly likely to be attempted, as he could escape up the numerous creeks further than the enemy were likely to follow, lest they should get trapped in some intricacy of the watery labyrinths, and fall into the hands of enemies lying in wait to receive them. His only fear was that he might be chased by the enemy in rowing boats, when there would undoubtedly ensue a severe struggle.

The *Dragon* floated past Thordsoe, and the ripple from its oars lapped the rock. She was steered through a reef which rose from a considerable depth to within a few feet of the low-water mark, and then the rowers sent her flying with long sweeps of their oars over a beautiful sheet of still water. Presently they paused, and the head of the boat was turned towards one of the many little creeks which opened on the right ; the rocks, which had been split asunder, rose abruptly on each side of an entrance so confined that the oars had all to be shipped in order to pass the channel. The boat dropped slowly through with the rising tide. Overhead a huge pine had fallen across the chasm, and the head leaned on a projection of the opposite crag. The water was perfectly clear, and its dark olive-green colour showed its vast depth. The men occasionally gave the vessel additional impetus by pressing their oars against the rocks on one side or the other. A hawk that had settled to roost, screamed, and, dashing out, rose and wheeled overhead. The sun was just setting, and a gleam shot in at the end of the rift, gilding the water; then it became fainter, and the last spark disappeared as the vessel floated into the broader expanse of a quiet land-girt bay.

' We may drop anchor here in perfect safety,' said Gregorius. ' Rolf, you and I had better go back to Thordsoe ; we can take a boat thence, and remain till the ships come up. Magnus had best stay in the *Dragon.* I wonder what has become of that fellow Thorarin. Whenever he is most wanted he disappears, and when least required he disturbs everyone with his noise. He will be rushing, with his usual impetuosity and lack of prudence, single-handed on the enemy and getting killed. Did any of you see him ?'

'I did,' said little Asmund. 'He went off in a boat, just before the ship sailed.'

'Which way, my child?' asked the bonder.

'Down, straight down the fiord,' replied the little boy.

'Well,' said Gregorius, with an air of relief, 'I suppose he has only gone to have a look about him, and watch until the ships come in sight. He knows, of course, where we are moored.'

'Yes,' added Rolf, 'and very angry the crack-brained lad was that we should flee before King Harald; he was all on fire to fight him. I shall not be in the least surprised if he gets us into danger now; he never can remain at rest.'

'You may take my word for it, master,' said a solemn man, who usually officiated as pilot to the *Dragon*, 'that Thorarin is now in Harald's power, and what will become of him, Heaven knows; though, to be sure, one may make a pretty shrewd guess. I know what King Harald *generally* does with his prisoners.'

'Why, Glum, what do you mean?' asked Rolf.

'Oh, nothing particular,' replied the man, dropping his jaw, and letting his face assume the most solemn and ghastly expression it was capable of. 'Only I have heard that King Harald of Konghelle allowed Asbiorn and his brother Nercid to choose their deaths, and that has been considered particularly liberal of him, giving them the choice that one should be hanged, and the other thrown down the Sarpsburg waterfall. Asbiorn chose to be thrown over the cataract, for that appeared to him to be the most dreadful of the two deaths, and he was the elder brother.'

'But, Glum,' said Magnus, 'you do not mean to say——'

'No, no,' interrupted the man, 'I do not believe that Thorarin has been treated thus; that, you see, was an exceptional case. The king generally kills those who oppose him by driving wedges of wood into their joints; but it is just possible that an exception may be made, Master Gregorius, with your son; we can but hope; though,' continued he, partly to himself, after a pause, looking over the bulwarks into the water, 'hopes are vain affairs after all, and things rarely turn out as we desire.'

'Glum,' exclaimed Magnus anxiously; 'what do you mean? You cannot be sure that Thorarin is taken.'

'Certainly not,' answered the pilot; 'not quite sure, oh no!—any more than, if I were to drop my cap, that it would touch the water; for who knows? some water-spirit might put forth an arm and carry it to land; but that would not be according to the *ordinary* course of nature. Well, Magnus, I will offer this,' and Glum's voice became sepulchral: 'if Thorarin has not his joints dislocated with wedges, you understand how I mean, like a crab's or lobster's ' —his jaw fell lower, he stretched forth his cold, bony hand and laid it on Magnus' shoulder, then leaning forward he spoke hoarsely into his ear—'Magnus, I'll eat the tiller!' Suddenly recoiling, he retreated to the further end of the ship, keeping his cold eye fixed on the youth; and till the darkness became sufficiently complete to hide all, wherever he turned, Magnus saw Glum's eye fastened on him, or received from him a complacent nod of satisfied consciousness that there was not the feeblest prospect of his word being falsified.

'Well, Rolf,' said Gregorius, going to the side of the deck, 'come with me to Thordsoe; throw me down a few things that we may want, and then jump down yourself, into the boat.'

In a moment or two the skiff darted into the deep shadow of the rocks, between which lay the entrance to the bay.

'I am vexed about Thorarin,' said Gregorius at length, pausing on his oar, as the boat glided out from the chasm; then he added, 'I hope that we shall have light enough to reach the islet; it is getting very dark now.'

'I know my way perfectly,' said Rolf; 'the darkness matters but little to me. But,' he added after a pause, 'I cannot conceive what can have made Thorarin row down the fiord, unless it were to keep a look-out upon the enemy.'

'And yet,' observed Gregorius, 'the lad has little fancy for remaining idly watching during several hours.'

The bonder's brother shrugged his shoulders and said, 'I can see no other reason for his having left us.'

'I wish we had remained, and I would have had him tied down in the hold; it would never do to leave him free—to go and do just what he liked. Well, the good God order all for the best!'

'Amen,' ejaculated Rolf, and a moment later, 'Mind, brother, we're just on the Bed of Violets; the tide is falling, do not pull deep.'

Gregorius' oar touched a point of the reef which stood near the surface.

'Are we over it?' he asked shortly after.

'Safe,' answered his brother; 'now back-water. That is it, her head is round, pull away lustily.'

In ten minutes the prow grated on the shingle, and Rolf and Gregorius leaped ashore.

'Let us get the boat up where it cannot be seen,' said the latter. 'You know best where to stow her.'

'She is safe here,' answered Rolf. 'Lend a hand, just to fasten her to this birch-tree.'

'If we get to the top of the cliff, we can rest the night there,' said Gregorius; 'and we shall have to watch thence to-morrow morning, as it commands both reaches of the fiord.'

'Follow me,' said Rolf; 'I know every inch of the way.'

The ground was broken and covered with underwood and stones, so that in the darkness it was a considerable time before the two could make their way through it, to the summit of the island; when there, they threw themselves on the ground.

Neither spoke, for, as if by mutual consent, both had made up their minds for a nap; when suddenly a faint splash on the opposite side of the main waters of the fiord drew Rolf's attention, so that, grasping his brother's arm tightly in his hand, he sat upright and listened.

'It is either a salmon, or else Thorarin is there,' said Gregorius in an undertone.

Rolf was not satisfied; he listened eagerly still, and both he and his brother could hear distinctly several voices speaking in a subdued tone; but the distance was so great that the sound was barely audible.

Presently Gregorius felt his brother press his arm tightly, and saw him point towards a part of the shore on the opposite side where the hills, dipping rather lower than at any other point, showed a mast standing out against the gray sky.

Rolf leaned towards his brother and whispered, 'They are there, moored already! I suppose they came up with the tide as we were getting into safe quarters ourselves. But they must have been rowing all day; they have passed Erling's farm and not injured it; that is very odd.'

'I see it all,' whispered Gregorius; 'they intend surprising Thordsâ-sund with the first dawn of morning, as it is the largest farm, and I am the wealthiest bonder on the fiord.'

Rolf nodded. 'And they are moored,' said he, 'just under the Skald's rock, out of sight of the farm.'

'I cannot see how many ships there are, can you?' asked Gregorius. 'Erling said there were three; I see one mast only;' he paused for a moment, and then said to himself: 'I wish that mad boy were safe in the *Dragon;* they may have captured him, for aught I know.'

'No fear of that yet,' said Rolf. 'Thorarin is like an eel; he would slip through their fingers if they tried to catch him.'

' You go to sleep, Rolf; I will watch the first part of the night, and then you shall take your turn whilst I get a doze.'

' A nap will do us no harm,' added Rolf; ' and the nights are not over-long just now;' and rolling himself on one side, he was asleep almost immediately.

' God's holy blessing be on us this night, and ever!' said Gregorius, rising to his feet; ' sleep sound, brother.'

CHAPTER V.

THORARIN AFLOAT.

Watching the Enemy

HEN the first streaks of morning began to appear, Rolf, who was on the watch, fixed his eyes intently on the point where he had seen the mast on the previous evening. As the light spread, he could perceive the dusky outlines of two ships riding at anchor in the little bay behind Skald's Point, and out of sight of Thordsâsund Farm. He woke his brother, and both examined the vessels closely.

In an hour the sun rose, and the golden light fell across the headland upon one of the ships which stood somewhat apart from the others, showing its quaint prow, carved and painted to represent an ungainly sea-bird which frequents the Northern shores.

'That is the *Puffin*,' whispered Rolf; 'I have heard of the boat. She is a fast sailer. Old Eric Greyskin built her.'

'There is some motion on board already,' said the bonder. 'Harald Gille is intending to attack the farm at once.' The brothers watched with great interest; at last Gregorius said, smiling: 'Rolf, it almost makes me laugh to think of the vexation of our enemies at finding us gone. Hlenni, undoubtedly, is the man who has urged them to make this rapid descent upon us.'

'You see,' observed Rolf, 'there are two ships only, and not three, as Erling supposed.'

A fresh breeze began to set in from the distant sea, ruffling the clear blue waters in lines, which, in the dim light sweeping down some eastern gully, quivered and sparkled as a sheet of gold-leaf.

The intention of Harald soon became evident. A large body of men was sent on shore at the nearest point, and was lost to sight in the woods; a little later and a boat from the *Puffin* was rowed up the fiord, passing the farm. No sooner had it doubled the headland, than a second boat was despatched in its wake, and was rowed leisurely past the farm; but was no sooner beyond it, than those on Thordsoe caught a glimpse of it being swiftly

propelled to a point on the side which those on land
were skirting.

'I do not exactly see what is their object,' said
Rolf.

'To me it is manifest,' replied Gregorius. 'The
king fears to attack Thordsâ-sund from the water,
lest we should take alarm in time, and muster in
sufficient numbers to oppose his landing. He has
accordingly sent his men along the shore to a point
above the farm, and the boats, which you saw were
thinly manned, will ferry them across, out of sight, to
assault the house from behind. I suspect the party
in the woods have carried Hlenni's boat with them.'

'One thing is apparent,' said Rolf: 'that the king
has brought only a handful of men with him, or he
would never have left his two ships with hardly a
soul on board.'

'Hlenni, I suppose, fell in with him some way up
the fiord, apart from his other ships, which must be
at the mouth, left to overawe those who might prove
troublesome, and has induced him to come on at
once without returning to get more hands.'

Such was the observation of Gregorius. There
ensued a pause, as both directed their eyes towards
the farm; nothing, however, was to be seen of the
enemy, and Rolf turned for a moment to scrutinize
the ships.

'Look there!' he exclaimed hastily, pointing
towards the shadow of some overhanging rocks and
trees on the same side of the fiord as himself. 'I
am sure there is a boat moving yonder.'

Gregorius gazed anxiously at the spot.

'It is just possible,' he muttered, 'that Hlenni may be skulking there, and going into all the creeks to see where the *Dragon* is moored—but no! that boat is going down, not up towards this inlet.'

'Strange!' exclaimed Rolf, after both had been watching with intense eagerness. 'There is such deep shadow that it is impossible to distinguish any-one; yet there are no oars being used. Those in it are pushing themselves along by the rocks.'

'Hark!' cried Gregorius, turning towards the farm, as a shout came thence; 'the enemy has surrounded Thordsâ-sund.'

In a moment the whole of the out-buildings were seen filled with men, the house was fired, and a small column of white smoke rose, and was dissi-pated by the sea-breeze. The brothers could see the work of destruction proceeding, the flames rapidly spreading, and range after range of wooden buildings catching fire.

The desertion of the place had evidently surprised the enemy, for there was a knot in consultation close by the beach. One of the number Rolf thought to be Hlenni, from the purple cloak which he wore, and which he believed he recognised as that found on Asmund's father.

Gregorius and Rolf saw that a large number of men were called off from the burning house, and only a few left, and that the man in the purple cloak led them away from it, by the road towards the mountain dairy.

'They are going to the sœter!'* gasped the bonder.

* An upland farm, occupied in the summer only.

'Would there were time to reach it before them, and warn the poor women to escape !'

'It is impossible !' said his brother ; 'do not think of such a thing. If our men there have been prudent, and kept a watch on the road, the poor creatures may have time to fly, even now.'

'It will be some hours before the wretches get there. God grant that Erling may be in the way !'

'Would it be of any use setting fire to the pine, and thus calling him to our assistance ? But—do look at that boat !'

Rolf directed Gregorius' eye to the little bark which had drawn his attention before ; it had left the shore, and was crossing the fiord. To all appearance there was no one in it, yet it advanced slowly towards the side where the ships lay.

After awhile, however, it seemed to be stationary. Gregorius calculated its progress by a point of rock beyond ; its only motion was at present the drift of the tide. Then, on the opposite side of the boat, an arm was thrust over the bulwark into the water, and slowly propelled the bark.

'Whoever it may be,' said Rolf, 'he is intent on avoiding detection from those at the farm. Do you see, he is crossing the narrow line of water visible from it ? In a moment more he will be round the bend of the fiord, beyond sight of Thordsâ-sund. There, look ! the fellow is sitting up and plying his oars.'

'Why, Rolf !' exclaimed Gregorius suddenly, 'I believe it is our Thorarin. What can the rash boy be after now ?'

'It *is* Thorarin,' cried Rolf, jumping to the edge
of the precipice. 'For once he will be of use; he is
going to light the pine.'

'I fear not,' said the bonder, with a sigh; 'he did
not hear of the signal. You keep your eye fixed on
him, brother; your eyes are keener than mine.'

'There is but one man on board each ship, as
far as I can see,' remarked the younger brother.
'Thorarin is close to them now, and the men on
them do not seem to have noticed him.'

'He has pushed his boat past the *Puffin*, has he
not?' asked the bonder.

'Yes, he has,' answered Rolf; and then with a
laugh he added, 'he is full of daring as a young
eagle. Do you see what he has done? Look, he is
alongside the *Serpent*, that ship nearest the shore,
and is climbing up the side.'

'Brave boy!' exclaimed Gregorius, beating his
hands together with excitement. 'Come, Rolf, into
the boat at once; he will require help;' and the
delighted father dashed through the bushes towards
the spot where the boat was moored. In far less
time than it had taken them to traverse the same
ground the preceding evening, the brothers had
reached their little skiff, thrown off the rope which
held it to the tree, and were floating from behind
Thordsoe.

'We must use discretion,' said Gregorius, 'and
keep near in shore till we pass the furthest point
within range of Thordsâ-sund.'

'Strike across this channel,' said Rolf. 'We can
carry the little boat along the shore in greater

secrecy; I chose the lightest we had in the *Dragon*.'

Gregorius agreed, saying: 'There is a path along the side, I believe.'

The boat grounded on the shore; it was speedily lifted on the brothers' shoulders, and borne through the thicket to the little path alluded to. In most places the trees were so thickly interlaced as not to afford them the slightest glimpse of farm or ships, but here and there they came out on a rock which commanded a view of both. Their path descended to a little cove, in which Thorarin had probably lain the night before. As they reached it, Rolf uttered an exclamation. The two ships were full in view before them, and from the *Long Serpent* was issuing a spiral jet of smoke.

'The lad has overpowered the guard and has fired it,' said Rolf. 'It is of no use attempting conceal- ment any longer; we must dash across to him. In with the boat!' and almost as soon as spoken the little vessel was dancing on the water, and the brothers had sprung in.

'Now give way!' exclaimed Gregorius vehemently, and the boat shot like a dart out of the bay. No one on the farm seemed to notice it, however; those who remained were scattered among the out- buildings searching for plunder, or too engrossed in their own pursuit to observe what was passing at a distance. In another moment it was hidden by the promontory, and was approaching the ships rapidly.

The smoke from the *Serpent* had grown thicker, and a lambent flame every now and then flickered in it.

GREGORIUS, ROLF, AND THORARIN ON BOARD THE 'PUFFIN.'

'It must be seen shortly from the farm,' said Rolf.
'Perhaps, also, it may recall those on their way to
the sœter.'

'I hope so!' exclaimed Gregorius. 'Well,
Thorarin,' he shouted, as he neared the ship
which was not on fire, and on which his own son
was now standing.

'Come, father,' cried the young man in reply;
'come quick, and help me to get the anchor of the
Puffin up.'

The boat sprang to the side, and the brothers
mounted to the deck. In but a short space of time
they had raised the anchor, and the head of the
vessel swung round down the fiord.

'Are there no men on board?' asked Gregorius.

'Of course there are,' answered Thorarin.
'Harald never left his ships unprotected; but the
watch were careless, and I got on deck unperceived.
Two men asleep, one half so. Him I knocked
down, and bound the others. There are three
men in the hold, fast as the enemy thought to
have us.'

'But you will not burn them alive—that is the old
pagan fashion, not becoming us Christians.'

'No, father,' said Thorarin. 'Help me, and we
will set them ashore, and they can see the *Long
Serpent* blaze, and it will help to wake them.'

Gregorius and Rolf assisted the young man in
moving the prisoners to the shore. The smoke was
becoming thick, and blinded them in the hold.
Then they left the *Long Serpent* to its fate, and
returned to the *Puffin*.

4

'Rolf,' said Gregorius, 'we must at once make up our minds what is to be done.'

'Get the sail up,' replied the one addressed. 'The wind has shifted some points since the break of morning, and will assist us in getting down the fiord.'

The flames, which had gained a complete mastery over the *Long Serpent*, seemed to have attracted the attention of the men at the farm, for repeated shouts were heard in that direction.

As the great sail, which the three now hoisted, flapped and then bellied out in the breeze, the *Puffin* rolled, and then shot out into the main waters, in full view of the farm.

A yell of anger rang from the distance over the water, and then the three sailors saw their enemies rush off through the wood towards the place where they had left their boats.

The flames from the burning ship had been carried by the wind towards the shore, the sparks had been borne as far as the old dead pine, near which the ship was moored, and a pale blue flame danced at the top; then some of the lesser forks crackled and flared up suddenly, sending down a shower of sparks; a small branch fell burning among the lower boughs and lighted them, a gush of yellow flame poured up from below, and in a moment more the whole tree was in a blaze, its great arms snapping, and dashing meteor-like into the water below.

Just then a yell came from the spot above Thordsá-sund Farm, where the boats, in which King Harald had crossed the fiord with his men, had been left, and presently the enemy were seen flying to the burning farm before Erling's farm servants, who were cutting them down, and driving them before them to the boats.

'Let us to shore and help!' exclaimed Thorarin, dashing to and fro on board the ship; 'I cannot remain idle here.'

'You shall not go ashore, boy,' said Gregorius; 'I have other work for you. Erling will not remain there long, he is far too wise; he knows that the main body of the rascals is up the mountains, and will be returning to the ships directly they catch sight of them from the heights, and see that the *Long Serpent* is flaming, and that the *Puffin* is in our hands. You may be sure Erling will be off directly he has sunk the boats. He must have mistaken the blaze from the ships for that of the pine, to have come so expeditiously.'

'Then, what do you intend doing, father?' asked Thorarin.

'I intend, first, dropping down the fiord as far as the next reach, opposite Erling's farm; then Rolf must go ashore in the boat, and strike across the hill to where the *Dragon* lies. Rolf, remember! the *Dragon* is to join the *Puffin*. There will be no danger coming into the fiord now; and we must both sail to-night out of the mouth——'

'But the king's fleet is there,' interrupted his brother.

'I doubt whether there be more than three ships,' replied Gregorius. 'The king would surely have brought more men into the fiord with him if he could have spared them, and the two vessels he did bring were not over-full.'

' Do you think this a better plan than remaining concealed?' asked Rolf.

' Undoubtedly,' replied his brother; ' the king would be sure to find us if we remained here, and I doubt if he would leave the fiord till he had cut us to pieces ; and, in the long-run, we should stand no chance against him. If we get out to sea, however, we shall have no need to fear, but can coast about till he has left, and then return and rebuild the farm.'

' It is certainly the best plan,' said Rolf, half to himself.

' And then,' pursued Gregorius, ' should King Magnus be defeated in the end, King Harald would never suffer us to live in peace, and I should leave for Iceland, where I have a farm, that comes to me by inheritance, which I have never visited.'

' What, Oræfa-dal?' asked Thorarin; ' Rolf has been there several times.'

The vessel was now beyond the range of Thordsâ-sund, and was slowly descending the reach to Erling's farm.

. Rolf was put on shore, and Thorarin brought the boat back to the *Puffin*. The wind dropped as the day advanced, so that the father and son made but little way, to their no great inconvenience, however, since they considered it best not to pass the dis-affected farms with the ship in its present condition, although there was no great fear of any interference from those who lived along the shores. The political changes of the country affected them too slightly to create any violent partisanship, living as they did so far North as to be seldom visited by the king, or called upon to own his authority in any other way than by paying the usual ' scatt,' or royal tax.

Magnus, the rightful sovereign, son of the old King Sigurd the Crusader, was a man who took but little pains to gain the affections of his lendermen and bonders ; hasty in temper, he refused the best advice, and would hear no opinion with patience which did not tally with his own. Consequently, he lost many of his best supporters, who, disgusted with his obstinacy, which was blindly precipitating him to ruin, left him, and retired as neutral spectators of the strife to their own farms. Harald Gille, an Irish upstart, who professed himself to be the brother of Sigurd, had so imposed on the old king as to have his relationship acknowledged, but had solemnly sworn to renounce all claims on the crown. No sooner, however, was the old king dead, than Harald cast his oath to the winds and claimed half the kingdom. Magnus resenting this claim, each party had recourse to arms, and at first Harald was defeated, and forced to take refuge in Denmark. The year preceding the opening of this tale he had been hanging about the coast, pillaging the farms of those who adhered to his rival, and calling Things whenever he had an opportunity, fascinating all by his graceful and courteous demeanour, which contrasted so strongly with that of his nephew.

Rumours had reached Thordsâ-sund early in the spring of a great battle in Viken, but the truth of the account was doubted. News travelled but sluggishly in Norway, and especially in the North, where all communication with the Southern provinces was cut off during the winter; so that when, with spring, it began to circulate, it was, at first in vague rumours, on which little reliance could be placed, as uncertain as the puff of wind preceding a gale, and blowing from quarters not always truly indicative of the direction of the master current.

CHAPTER VI.

ON THE DEEP.

S the day declined, the father and son cast many an anxious glance up the fiord, and it was with heartfelt delight that they caught sight of the gilded *Dragon's* head, gleaming from behind a belt of pines; and when, with a few sweeps of the oars, she came alongside of the *Puffin*, they greeted her with hearty cheers. Gregorius' first question, naturally, was about the farm, and the motions of the enemy.

'The whole body is there,' said Rolf; 'I saw Hlenni on the shore. It is evident that those in pursuit returned to the farm before reaching the sœter, and that Erling has destroyed the boats, so that they cannot recross the fiord. You may be sure that Hlenni will lead them by land to Guttorm's-dal, and give the king his own ships.'

'You would have laughed, father,' said Magnus,
'to have seen Harald, when the brave old *Dragon*
came out, with its head blazing in the sun, and the
sail up, for we hoisted just behind Thordsoe ; he and
all his men rushed down and looked as astonished
as if they had a vision of the æsir ; and I saw the
king walking vehemently up and down like a caged
beast, furious to be at us, and unable.   I knew him
by his height and splendid headpiece.'

The good old bonder chuckled.

'Thorarin, my boy,' said he; 'we owe this all to
you ; he is a happy father who can look on his son,
and, with a single heart, thank God that he is his
own flesh and blood !   If we come safely through
this matter, and float in the broad sea, beyond the
reach of our foes, I will give you my good old sword,
Hneitir, and may you ever reverence God as your
ancestors have done !'

Thorarin's dark eyes flashed with pleasure ; he
clasped his father's hand, and said, ' Let me swim to
the first ship of the enemy we meet with, and cut my
way from stern to prow, and then swim to you again.'

Gregorius smiled, and, turning to Rolf, said :
' Brother, let us man our ships at once, and get
down towards the sea.'

Half the crew of the *Dragon* was drafted to the
Puffin ; this occasioned no inconvenience to the
former ship, as it had been filled, while lying concealed, with most of the able-bodied men on the
farm, and the numbers in it had consequently been
more than were necessary for the management of the
vessel. Gregorius entrusted the *Dragon* to the charge

of Rolf and Magnus, keeping Thorarin with himself on board the *Puffin*.

It had been a matter of satisfaction to all to observe that, as the sun set, the few clouds which had been straying about had settled together, while others rolled up from the horizon, over-casting the sky, so that there was every promise of a dark night. The wind blew fresher, and as the boats neared the mouth of the fiord, they began to heave with the swell of the distant ocean. Darkness at last settled in, and they advanced steadily. On the shores were some straggling lights, showing that the number of farms nearest the coast was more considerable than higher inland. Before long they caught sight of the smouldering embers of Folga Farm; then the breeze from the sea blew in their faces fresh, and redolent of sea-weed, and they could hear the roar of the waves about Folga Point and its kelp-covered reefs. The clouds overhead had become more dense, so that the blackness deepened, and the ships of Harald Gille, at the mouth of the fiord, were perfectly invisible, till the *Puffin*, which led the way, ran close by one.

'The *Puffin!*' shouted Gregorius in answer to a challenge from the other, and the ships swept past into the darkness. The *Dragon* rolled by, and was doubtless mistaken by the enemy for another of their own ships: of the other vessels, neither boat saw any signs, they were probably riding some distance apart. All danger was now over, and the *Dragon* and *Puffin* stood out to sea.

The short spring night soon passed, and when

morning dawned, the mountainous coast lay along the horizon, like a bank of fog, before which spread the wide sweeps of sea, frothing in the fresh gale which broke the clouds up, and drove them about, glittering in the splendour of the risen sun. The two boats coasted south, and on the following day Gregorius ran up a fiord in the *Puffin*, to visit a lenderman of his acquaintance, in order to gather some certain information respecting the proceedings of King Magnus. The news he heard was sufficiently decisive to compel him to frame plans at once for leaving Norway. A battle had been fought during the winter, at Viken, in which Harald had utterly defeated his nephew, and had put out his eyes; it was said that King Magnus had retired to a monastery, hopeless of ever regaining his crown. This report was confirmed by others, so that no manner of doubt with respect to its authenticity could exist.

Gregorius now regretted not having submitted quietly to Harald; but Thorarin insisted vehemently that it would have been useless to have done so, as Hlenni had doubtless informed the king of his being a violent partisan of Magnus, or he would have offered terms before attacking the farm.

It was evident to all that it was completely out of the question to remain in Norway, and Gregorius determined on running up the fiord, after Harald had left it, and removing all the effects which had been secreted, his daughter, and some of the farm women, and then sailing at once for Oræfa-dal, his Icelandic property.

For days the weather continued beautiful, and the *Puffin* and *Dragon* kept well out to sea, so as to be beyond any chance of falling in with the king's ships; occasionally they would approach the land, gleaning tidings of Harald; and at length, having heard of his progress up the coast, and back again towards Viken, the two vessels re-entered the fiord, and sailed up the lovely reaches, till Thordsoe and the blackened ruins of the farm hove in sight. As they passed each homestead, every inhabitant turned out, and ran down upon the beach to watch them, the story of their exploit having got wind and excited the curiosity or sympathy of the people along the shore. At Erling's farm a boat put off and came alongside of the *Dragon*. The good old farmer congratulated Rolf on his escape, and agreed with him that the only step advisable was to leave Norway at once. His own farm had been left un-injured, as his participation in the occurrence at Thordsâ-sund had not been discovered; the attack he had made, and his sinking the boats, having been attributed to some of Gregorius' farm servants.

It took some days before all preparations for departure were accomplished, and then, Ingibjorg with her maidens and a sufficient number of men having been received on board, the two boats descended the fiord and put to sea.

'Well, Glum,' said Magnus, with a smile, ' you have not fulfilled your promise of eating the tiller.'

' Thorarin did not fall into the power of the king ; but wait awhile !' replied the pilot, nodding his head with a self-confident air.

'For what?' asked Magnus.

'We are going to Iceland,' said the man solemnly.

'And what of that?' inquired the youth.

'There are boiling springs there,' murmured Glum, with a cadaverous smile; 'people *often* fall into them, and are slowly cooked. I never told you of my uncle's cousin's brother, did I?'

'Never,' replied Magnus; 'was he an Icelander?'

'Yes,' said Glum gloomily. 'Poor fellow! he was very much attached to a beautiful girl who lived near the Eyafialla, which often erupts boiling mud—we are going to reside there. Well, one of these outbursts, which are happening continually, carried away the maiden's house and herself while haymaking. Her lover heard of the accident, ran to the spot, and chanced on the corpse of his betrothed, which was floating in the boiling mud; then,' continued Glum, with a look of animation near akin to joy, 'he seized her, that he might clasp the dear remains to his lacerated bosom, but—she ran through his fingers like melted butter!'

Magnus shuddered, and inquired whether this terrible incident were really true.

Glum replied with a hollow moan, 'A spoonful, Magnus, is preserved as a family relic.'

CHAPTER VII.

THE BAD SUB-DEACON.

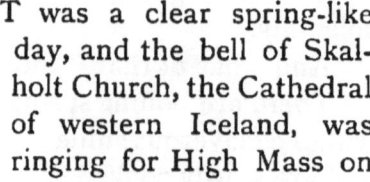

T was a clear spring-like day, and the bell of Skalholt Church, the Cathedral of western Iceland, was ringing for High Mass on the festival of the Ascension. The houses and church were all of wood; round the latter was a broad space of turfy burial-ground, and to the west a patch of vivid green meadow, in which gyrated knots of horses, the head of each tied to the tail of the other, so as to form a living circle wheeling here and there, as the beasts endeavoured to advance in quest of fresh grass. The grim lava-rocks around were enlivened with patches of the same brilliant green turf, but towards the south-west they were wilder; the gleams of grass-land were replaced by black sandy deserts, and ridge after ridge of desolate rocks arose about the distant triple cone of Heckla, which shone a most dazzling white. Near the church were groups of people awaiting the procession from the neighbouring college; some lounged against the walls gossiping, others watched the horses, whilst the most devout were on their knees in the porch. Within the monastery the procession was forming.

'Brother Pâl,' said the precentor, 'you start the Introit. Now, boys, no whispering among yourselves; walk steadily and behave well. Take care not to draggle the ends of your albs in the mud in crossing that dirty bit by the gate. Tuck them up like this,' and the worthy monk lifted his cape and alb, so as to show his massive feet and ankles. 'And, dear brother Swerker, you must not sing quite so loud; you put the whole choir flat.'

'No one relishes my singing here,' answered Swerker, a round, merry-looking man, with a laugh; 'and yet, when I pay a visit home, my good mother and sisters are continually requesting me to sing a quida* or even a drapa. Indeed,' he added with a cough, 'I believe I composed one myself, but the good folks, having heard it once, never asked for it again.'

'Well, Swerker,' said the precentor, nudging him, 'I'll let you sing it to me one of these days, having previously stopped my ears with tallowed flax; but

* A quida was a short song or lay, the drapa a longer composition.

be still now, we are just beginning to start, and I
cannot keep the boys quiet if you talk.'

'But you have not got the banner down yet,'
retorted brother Swerker.

'Master Sacristan, have you been asleep? Where
is the blessed Olaf banner?' exclaimed the precentor.

'It is coming,' replied the sacristan, 'I have
ordered it to be dusted a little; it was in a frightful
state.'

As he spoke, a boy brought the banner into the
passage where the fraternity were assembled.

'Now, then,' exclaimed the precentor, who acted
as master of the choir, and had the arrangement of
all the processions, 'you who are deacon and sub-
deacon to-day, get into your places. Thurifer,
mind there are no fish-bones in the censer to-day.
Brother Swerker, do get your cope to sit better.
Why, bless the man, he has put it on inside out!
Change it quick, we are desperately late. Eric, you
take the banner; and you two boys, John and Alf,
hold the leading-strings, and don't wipe your noses
with the tassels. Now, Swerker, if your hair is not
all ruffled, as if you had just got out of bed! Could
you not have changed your cope without pulling it
over your head? My dear brother, do be a little
more careful of personal appearance.'

'I am not going to hold the banner,' exclaimed
Eric, a fiery young sub-deacon; 'it is not my place;
give it to one of the acolytes.'

'Eric,' exclaimed the precentor from the end of
the procession, 'take the banner directly.'

'I will not touch it,' replied the youth vehemently;

' I am not going out of my proper place. It is to
insult me that you tell me to take it.'

' I am sure he never thought of such a thing,'
groaned Swerker.

' I'll answer for myself, please,' said the precentor.
' Take it at once, young cub.'

Eric folded his arms contemptuously, and, leaning
back against the wall, said : ' Cub indeed ! I am
better born than any of you. Serve a set of low-
born knaves I will not. Give me a sub-deacon's
task and I will do it ; I can sing the gradual as well
as any other, and better, but carry a banner I will
not. Give it to one of the children.'

' Did you ever hear the like ?' cried Swerker in
amazement ; and, as the choir children began to
crowd round, he said : ' Eric, do as you are bid ; see
what an example you are setting these boys. The
bishop is waiting, we must go on and meet him. I
shall speak to him about you if you do not act as
you are bid, and he will disgrace you.'

' And what care I ?' exclaimed the deacon, his
wild dark eyes sparkling. ' Let the bishop do his
worst !'

Swerker, who had been gaping with astonishment,
now rolled his lusty body forward, and took the
banner in his powerful hand.

' Now, then, Eric,' said he indignantly, ' take this
at once.'

' Never,' replied the boy resolutely.

Swerker raised his huge arm, and at a blow
knocked him over. Cat-like, the young clerk was
on his feet again, had sprung on the old man, had

ERIC REFUSES THE BANNER.

5

wrenched the banner from him, and dashed it on the ground. The furious boy leaped and trampled on it as if it were an object of his greatest abhorrence.

' I will not hit you !' he yelled at Swerker. ' You fisherman's son, I despise you too much to strike you !'

' Eric,' groaned the priest, striving to pick up the banner, at the head of which was a gilded cross, ' for the love of Heaven do not tread on the holy sign !'

' Take it, then !' cried the youth, spurning cross and banner from him. ' Go on to your church ; I have had enough of you all. Methinks a leper-house were preferable to this asylum of sanctified idiots. Farewell for ever !'

He stood for a moment looking on them all, his body quivering with rage, his hands clenched, his face flushed crimson, while a vein on his forehead turned black and stood out as if about to burst. Then with a leap he burst the door open, and tearing his alb off him, hurled it, in shreds, back into the passage. Plunging forth upon the turf, he darted away among the lava crags.

The precentor calmly advanced from the rear, and, lifting the tattered alb, said deliberately :

' I shall make his mother pay for this. Cathedral property shall not be destroyed with impunity.'

' He is possessed,' said Swerker with a sigh. ' If he had remained only a little longer I would have exorcised him. Poor lad ! do you think it were any good my going after him now ?'

. ' No, no, brother,' said the infirmarer, catching

him by the sleeve. 'Let the boy alone, he will return when his fit is over. I wish I could have given him a dose of borko-bonda* root.'

'I wish,' emphatically observed the precentor, 'that I could swinge him well with a stick covered with buds. If not with that, I would borrow the crosier from the bishop.'

'Alas!' sighed the sacristan, 'bishop and people have been waiting, the blessed Olaf knows how long; and we must go without the beautiful banner. If it cannot be cleaned it will really break my heart. Oh, the wicked youth!'

'Boys, to your places,' exclaimed the precentor, 'and mind you accent the first notes of the mediation and cadence, and the alternate notes after those, or—— Swerker, where are you running to? That is not your place.'

'I am so confused,' apologized the good old man. 'Dear! alack the day, to think that my eyes should behold such a dreadful Berserker rage within these walls! I never would have believed that the devil could have got in here. You must put up a big cross, brother sacristan, over the gate, and I shall paint over it the adjuration to the devils in St. Mary Magdalene. I will look it out in the Gospels after service.'

'Move on now,' said the precentor loudly. 'Brother Pâl, begin the processional, if you please. Alf, hold the door open till we are all out, and then scamper back into your place. Steady!'

'*Omnes gentes, plaudite,*' chanted Pâl; the choir

* Borko-bonda, the spotted orchis (*Orchis maculata*).

caught it up, and moved out of the house. On passing the next they were joined by the bishop, who walked last; the men outside the church removed their caps, and after the procession had entered the cathedral, closed in behind, and filled the nave.

We leave the bishop at the altar, on which, in place of candles, burned lamps of seal-oil, and follow the bad sub-deacon in his escape across the desert of Mount Heckla, to his home on the southern coast of the island near the base of the Oræfa and Skapta Jökulls.

And here, before proceeding any further, it will be well to explain to the reader what a Jökull is. A Jökull, or, as we would pronounce it, Yökull, is a mountain clothed in ice and snow, that slide down in every direction in perpetual glacier. In Switzerland the glaciers occupy high valleys in the mountains, but in Iceland they cover the entire mountain, which is completely clothed in an icy crust, over which, each winter, fresh snow accumulates. The rivers flowing from these glacier mountains are of the colour of milk-and-water, as they hold much undissolved snow in suspense.

As the young man advanced, the scenery around became wilder; on the banks of the Thjorsâ he paused; that huge, turbulent stream was too deep and rapid to be swum. He therefore ran along the bank towards the ferry; the boat was on the shore where the ferryman had left it while he went to church. The youth sprang in, and rowed across in a slanting direction, the violence of the stream sweeping him far below the landing-place on the other side. No sooner was he safe on the bank than he flung the boat loose, and with a kick sent it back into the current, where it whirled round, drifted down, and finally stranded on a sand-bank in the middle of the stream. Before him the rocks rose again, and beyond glimmered the icy backs of the Tindfialla and Eyafialla Jökulls, broken here and there with black rents or cones of pumice. At times he had to clamber over some wall of vitrified rock, which had splintered in cooling, perforated on the summit with crater-like openings, formed by huge lava blisters which had burst, and in the cavities of which lay beds of green sod; then a patch of grass-land would intervene, and then another swarthy ridge of lava. On his right lay cones of red slag, one of which was puffing forth, with a whistling sound, small jets of steam. His feet were galled with the rocks, and fagged with the pumice sand. At times the rocks varied: some were ash-gray, some brown, some denser, others more porous, according to their age; sometimes stripes of red clay would intervene as strata, and now and then the way passed under Trölhladir, or ranges of basaltic columns, supposed by the islanders to be the abodes of dwarfs. Eric spent the night in a natural lava cavern, and appeased his hunger on the stalks of wild angelica, which covered the swampy land near. The following morning he advanced south, crossing several streams, keeping the Eyafialla Yökull full in view. This glacier mountain began now to exhibit its magnificent proportions, shining in the morning light like a vast sea of snow, studded with islands, heaved up between heaven and earth, and tilted on one side. In places where the glacier descended into the valleys the snow was gray with the particles of sand which had mingled with it, but higher up the ice showed its broken edges, light green, frosted over with silver. Eric felt thoroughly weary and hungry; seeing a column of steam rising near him, he turned aside, and found a boiling spring, which broke from a circular basin of calcareous deposit, through a tube in which the water was bubbling. Every now and then it rose and filled the basin, beautifully encrusting the grass around it. At regular intervals also the spout shot to the height of several feet, sending up a cloud of steam, and then sank rapidly down the bore. Fortunately for the sub-deacon, a poor sheep had lost its way in the desert, and was cropping the scanty grass near the spring. Eric lost no time in capturing it, and, having knocked its brains out with a stone, threw it over the bore of the small geyser. It simmered here for some time, dancing up with the rising water, and was then left dry. The jet repeatedly flung the parboiled carcase over the basin rim, but Eric threw it back until sufficiently cooked. Even then it made no excellent meal, for portions of the body were over-boiled, while others were half raw.

On the following day Eric took the Shaptâ Jökull as a landmark, making for it with renewed strength and spirits.

As he approached, farms began to appear, and

beautiful meadows refreshed his eyes, wearied with the swarthy lava rock.

At length the huge Oræfa Jökull towered before him, and the sea glimmered on his right, the intermediate distance being intersected with rivers pouring from the snow mountains and glaciers, spreading rapidly, and forming the large sheet of water called Gnupsvatn, patched with sandy chains of islands covered with wild corn. Eric's heart beat fast as he came within sight of Hraunvellir, with its pleasant pasture fields and Tûn;* the belt of coppice which surrounded the hill-tops; the old chasms in the brown tufa filled in, and becoming gradually covered with turf; the white boat-house; and the little skiff, dancing on the clear blue water, as the fishermen were coming to shore.

The streams from the Sand-fell glacier were passed, the last hill was climbed; and before sunset, two days after his having left Skalholt, the young sub-deacon burst into his mother's house, and rushed into her arms. Eric strongly resembled his mother; from her he had inherited the wild, tiger-like eyes, and the dark vein in the forehead, which swelled and blackened with passion. She was a tall and stately matron, with a face which, though aged, still bore the traces of great beauty of a commanding style. Her dark hair was almost fiercely bound back beneath her tall head-dress; her eyebrows were beautifully arched, but when she frowned they contracted into a large dark band, so that the effect

* The out-buildings and paddocks surrounding a farm; in parts of England these still bear the name of *town*.

produced by the brow, when she was angry, was repulsive in the extreme. Her lips were thin, and the chin pointed; her cheeks hollow and pallid. She listened quietly to the story Eric told her, of his escape from Skalholt monastery, and only interrupted him now and then with an emphatic 'Good!' When the recital was over, she turned towards her son with a strange look, half as if about to bite him, half as if to embrace him, and said, 'I am glad you are come home; I am glad. Come out of the door at once;' and she rose from her seat and walked from the room, then, turning, cast a fierce glance of anger back, because Eric had not risen and followed her at once.

'Look about,' she said, sweeping the horizon with her outstretched finger; 'you see the whole of the farm-lands from here. All but the hamlet over the spur of the Yökull is yours.'

'But where is my father?' asked Eric vehemently.

'Dead—dead!' exclaimed his mother, in a wild, convulsed voice, as her brows knit and the vein swelled and blackened. 'The sun is setting,' added she; 'come out on that crag, and you shall hear all.'

To the south of the farm rose a small hill of obsidian; that is to say, of rock that has been vitrified, so that it resembles black bottle-glass. The hill was covered for the most part with grass. Some way up the side protruded a mass of rock; on this Eric and his mother Gudruna seated themselves.

'Now, mother,' said the youth, 'tell me what has happened to my father. I have heard nothing of him since you sent me word that he had gone to

Norway, last autumn, and had taken my brother with him, to place him as foster-child to some jarl.'*

'That was not all he went for,' replied Gudruna; 'he went to visit Sira Gregorius of Thordsâ-sund. Oræfa-dal Farm belongs to him, and your father went to purchase it.'

'Well,' said Eric vehemently, 'go on at once, mother!'

'Here!' exclaimed the matron, tearing a letter fiercely from her bosom, 'if there were light enough, son, you should read it; but I know its purport well: it comes from a bonder, Hlenni by name, at whose house Onund stayed before going to Thordsâ-sund. Hlenni declares that Gregorius and your father fell out about the purchase of the farm, that from words they came to blows, and that Onund was killed. Eric, my son!' hissed Gudruna through her teeth, 'he was killed.'

'By the holy saints!' cried the bad sub-deacon, leaping to his feet. 'No, I will not swear by them; by the old evil spirit of our pagan forefathers—by thee, Surtur!† I swear, mother, to revenge him.'

'That is well, my son,' said the widow; 'listen to me. Eric, why does Hlenni write to me about your father's murder? Why does he not go up, at night, and fire Thordsâ Farm, and drive Gregorius back into the flames, if he be a friend of Onund? Hlenni is a coward; but thanks for his news, or I should never have known how my husband died.'

* 'Jarl,' a title from which our word 'earl' is derived.
† Surtur, the same as the Saxon Satur, from whom our Saturday is derived. In Iceland coal is called Surtur-brand, or devil's fuel.

'Mother,' interrupted Eric, 'what has become of Asmund?'

'The letter says he is killed, too; perhaps Gregorius feared that the child would tell of him, and murdered it.'

Gudruna threw herself back on the rock, and was silent for some while; at last she laughed hoarsely to herself.

'Mother, what are you thinking of?' asked Eric.

'Hush, boy!' replied she, waving him off with her hand, 'I am thinking of Thordsâ-sund on fire, and Gregorius leaping among the flames. Eric, shut your eyes and fancy him falling in a great heap among the red ashes!' and she uttered a wild laugh like a scream.

'Mother,' exclaimed the young man, clutching her hand, 'I swear to you truly, though your eyes may never see it, yet your ears shall hear of it. I will go to Norway at once and have vengeance.'

'I will go, too,' said Gudruna impetuously; 'I cannot rest till I have seen it.'

'No, mother,' replied Eric, 'you shall not go. I will do myself all that is necessary. Do you doubt my courage?'

'Never—you have sworn to revenge.'

As she spoke, a low roll, like thunder, passed far beneath their feet in the bowels of the earth, echoing through vast subterranean vaults, and followed by a rattle like chariot wheels over a pavement.

'Surtur hears us, mother!'

'And answers,' was Gudruna's reply.

CHAPTER VIII.

COASTING.

The Giant Rocks.

THE *Dragon* and the *Puffin* were slowly nearing Iceland. The weather in general had been calm, and the sea but slightly agitated.

Gregorius trusted principally to the superior nautical skill and knowledge of his brother, who, having been twice to Iceland before, was fairly acquainted with the disposition of the island ; and he therefore followed in his wake. For the last few days of the voyage the men had rowed harder than before, as Rolf feared a storm, on account of the gradual break-up of the weather and the increasing swell of the sea.

'I shall be glad when we get to land,' said Asmund, who was sitting beside Magnus on deck; 'I am tired of the water.'

'We shall soon be in Iceland,' observed Magnus ; 'I have been looking at the horizon for some while, and am sure that I can see a line of snow-capped mountains.'

'Where ?' cried the little child eagerly.

Magnus pointed in the direction, and Asmund instantly exclaimed that he saw quite distinctly the sun shining on the snow.

'Uncle Rolf sees it also,' said Magnus; 'look how he is bending his eyes northward.'

'Yes, that is Iceland,' murmured Glum behind him ; 'the place which is regularly turned inside out in ten years, what with volcanoes, boiling springs, and earthquakes.'

'I am heartily glad to see it, Glum,' said Magnus, smiling.

'Well, well, that is like enough,' observed the pilot ; 'but you don't know to what you are going. I do, for I have been there before, and, thanks be to the blessed Olaf, I am alive to say so.'

'You cannot frighten me about it,' said Magnus.

'That is just what my uncle's great aunt said, when told what sort of an island she was coming to settle in, and she suffered accordingly,' murmured Glum.

' How ?' asked Asmund, looking up.

' Never mind how, my child,' answered Glum sternly; 'only let me warn you never to drink geyser water, or it will turn you into stone.'

' But how is one to know geyser water from any other ?' asked the child.

Glum shrugged his shoulders.

'It turned my uncle's great-aunt's inside into stone; after that she had no relish for any food—for why ? Because her tongue was stone, her palate was stone, her throat stone, and she never could digest anything at all. So she died—outside flesh, inside stone.'

Glum smiled grimly, and walked away.

' We have drifted rather to the west,' said Rolf, coming up. ' Do you see the Troll in the offing ?'

'That rock ?' asked Magnus, pointing to a blue column on the horizon.

' Yes,' replied his uncle. ' Man has never scaled it. They say that a giant who lived in Iceland determined to find how deep he could wade in the sea; he stepped off the Ranger Sand, upon the Westmann Islands, and then down into blue water up to his middle. " There is not another mortal dare venture so deep as this," said he. He waded on, till, far beyond him, he beheld the Mealsack Rock, and thought it must be the head of another giant who had ventured across the ocean from Jotunheim, on his way to occupy Iceland. Then he was alarmed, for, " This other giant," thought he, " must be bolder and greater than myself; and therefore farewell to my empire in Iceland!" His heart sank within his breast and turned to stone. There, you see him yonder—become a rock from fear.'

'I think he must have drunk of the petrifying spring, Glum,' remarked Magnus, looking askance at the pilot, who had sidled up again.

'Now, Magnus,' continued Rolf, 'remember the giant when you dread a distant evil. Had he waded on a little further, he would have seen that the dark object before him was no giant's head rising out of the waves, but only the Mealsack Rock.'

In course of time the ships neared the Troll. It was a tall rock rising some hundreds of feet above the water level. About the base hung long streamers of green seaweed, while above, on ledges, squatted rows of white-breasted puffins. Around the head a flight of gannets was wheeling and screaming; while from among them, soaring high, rose the skua-gull. Every now and then the highway robber of the air made a dash at some gorged seabird carrying off a fish, made him drop it, and caught and appropriated the falling spoil. Most lovely were the tern with their coral-red legs and beaks and their jaunty black caps, and the kittiwakes with their soft, silvery plumage and greenish beaks. Here there fluttered the great ivory gull, like a portion of snow detached from the glacier mountains, and sent adrift on the wind. The waves muttered and foamed around the base of the black crag, forming dangerous eddies. Both ships kept at some distance, and before long the precipitous rock lessened in their wake.

A distant headland-bluff, along whose base the foam of the surge was faintly visible, came in sight,

and then the twilight of a summer night closed in, if
that can be called twilight when the amount of light
is no more reduced than by a cloud drawn over the
sky in Southern climes. Of night there is none. Of
real twilight none. A little diminution of light for a
brief period—that is all.

When the sun rose again after its brief withdrawal,
it gilded the red cones of Eyafialla rising out of
snow; the black needle rocks bristled out of the
waves as the boats neared the shore. On the highest
point of one of these a huge cormorant was stretch-
ing its neck to stare at the passing ships. The
Skaptâ and Oræfa Jökulls next towered up on the
horizon; they were visible but for a short while, and
then volumes of mist rolled down their flanks and
veiled the distant prospect. The wind had risen,
and the sea began to froth about the keels of the
ships. The rough headlands of basalt, their bases
lashed with foam, between Reynir and Skeiderâ
sands were left behind. In front rose the promontory of Ingolfhofdi, and on the following morning, as
a squall burst over the coast, the two boats entered
the gap in the Breidamark sand-bar, and were in still
water.

A short distance inland opened the pleasant vale
Oræfa-dal, which wound to the roots of the glacier-
mountain from which it took its name; and it was
in this valley that the homestead belonging to Gregorius was planted.

We must reserve a description of the place for the
following chapter.

CHAPTER IX

ORÆFA-DAL AT LAST.

Ingib-
jorg.

THE author feels a nervous apprehension that his readers may have been wondering all this while when they were to be introduced to the place the name of which heads his story. Yet he has the inward satisfaction of knowing that any censure which on that account may have been passed upon him is unmerited, since Oræfa-dal has, from the first chapter to the present one, been the key-note on which his varying chords have been constructed.

Oræfal-dal was a broad, cheerful vale at the time of the year when its proprietors now visited it

smiling with its vivid green fields, on which
numerous herds of cattle or flocks of sheep pastured,
or with its less emerald meadows, whose grass was
flowering and ready to cut.   Half-way up the height
ran belts of wood—coppice *we* should call it, for in
Iceland no tree reaches eight feet in height; and
above these shot crags of dark tufa.   To the north
rose the vast mountain glacier, Oræfa, a mass of
snow; towards the west it sloped downwards and
trailed its white fringe along some low heights, till,
nearing the sea, it swelled into a considerable hill of
ice, designated as the Hnapavellir glacier, a name
derived from a blotch of lava, like a button, in the
centre of its fields of stainless white.   From this
point the hills dropped in gentle stream-covered
descents to the Breidamark bay.   A white turbulent
river shot from the roots of the Oræfa, and poured
down the vale, whirling along with it masses of
discoloured ice, its shores streaked with black
volcanic sand.   At certain seasons it was passable
by fording; at others no communication could be
had with its further side.   Some way up the slopes
on the western bank stood the farm which Gregorius
had inherited through his wife, and which he had
now come to occupy.

The bad weather, which had for so many days
been threatening, broke along the coast in gales and
heavy scuds of rain, only after awhile abating into
days of continuous drizzle, which were spent by the
family in arranging the articles of furniture in their
new abode.   The *Dragon* and *Puffin*, which rode in
perfect safety within the Breidamark sand-bar, were

rapidly unladen, and their contents carried up to the farm.

Gregorius congratulated himself on the hay being uncut, and consequently standing little prospect of injury from the rain. Rolf had, as previously stated, been to Iceland before, collecting rent for his brother, so that he was well acquainted with the locality, and was of the greatest assistance in procuring all necessaries.

The first excitement of furnishing their new quarters kept all in good spirits ; but after a few days, when this had abated, and the rain continued to patter without, when leaks became only too apparent in roofs and doors, and when the wood which Rolf had cut would only smoulder, a feeling of dejection gradually spread over the whole party, and at last ended one dreary evening with Ingibjorg bursting into tears on her father's breast.

'Do not give way, daughter,' said the bonder, stroking her forehead. 'No doubt but that it is a sad thing to leave an old home ; still, there are pleasures in settling in a new land, and there may be beauties in a fresh country in which the old may have been deficient.'

'This is the best fire I ever saw in Iceland,' murmured Glum, who was crouching over the hearth, trying to kindle a flame among some damp twigs, 'and I've been in Iceland before, with Rolf.'

'I never shall like this island,' whimpered Ingibjorg ; 'there is rain, rain, and nothing else.'

'Nothing else,' echoed Glum, from the fire. 'My uncle's brother's son lived ten years in this country, and never once got dry all that while, till he tumbled down a volcano, and then went off in a puff of ash.'

'There!' exclaimed Ingibjorg, still crying, 'you hear what Glum says. I don't know how I shall ever live here. And then—the cold must be so dreadful in winter, I should think.'

'Horrible,' moaned Glum. 'My uncle's brother-in-law, one winter, went outside the house-door, and froze just as he was standing.'

'How very terrible!' gasped Ingibjorg.

'Very,' sighed Glum grizzly. 'One cuts one's meat with a chopper.'

'Glum,' said Gregorius, 'do not say such things; you know that they are untrue.'

The pilot shrugged his shoulders, and looked out of the corner of his eyes at the girl with a solemn expression, intended to convey the impression that truth was a thing which he intensely appreciated.

'Go to Thorarin, friend,' said the bonder; 'tell him to see about making some nets. You and he may very well work upon them during this wretched weather, and we shall want them speedily.'

The man growled and left the hall.

'I wish, father, that we might go to some other country; I know that I shall not like this,' said Ingibjorg.

'That cannot be helped, child,' replied Gregorius. 'God has placed our lot here, and it is our duty to be cheerful in it; but let me warn you not to believe all that Glum says. He never looks on anything in a sunny aspect; nothing is lively to him except some misfortune or calamity, and as for his uncles and

aunts, I do not believe one word which he tells
about them.'

'I wish you had not brought him, then,' sobbed
the girl.

'Daughter,' answered the old man, 'a truer and
better-hearted servant never lived, and we must
know how to put up with, and bear gently, the
foibles of our fellow-creatures. Now go and see
about supper being got ready.'

Ingibjorg fretfully obeyed. As she went, Magnus
caught her arm, and, leading her into the passage,
said :

'I wish, sister, that you would try to cheer our
father a little ; he feels this change very much, so
do not let us add to his trouble by being discontented
ourselves.'

'You mind your own self,' answered the girl
sharply. 'I like hearing sermons only on Sundays,
and then not from you ;' and she walked proudly
away.

Later in the evening, when supper was ready and
the fire at length coaxed into a blaze with some bits
of driftwood which had been found in an out-house,
the spirits of the party gradually revived, and the
conversation assuming a livelier tone than was
compatible with his enjoyment, Glum moped in a
corner and foreboded doleful things.

Magnus, who seemed bent on cheering the others,
had just finished a 'quida' in praise of Iceland, when
Thorarin entered, bringing a stranger with him.

'Here, father,' said he, 'I found this good priest
coming to visit you ; we met some way down the

stream, whither I had gone, tired of remaining within.'

' My name is Swerker,' said the stranger, coming forward. ' I live in the Cathedral College of Skal-holt, but have come down on particular business of rather a sad nature to this part of the island. This being my native district, on hearing of the arrival of settlers from Norway, I thought it only right to visit you, and offer my services, if I can be of assistance to you in any way.'

Gregorius thanked the priest cordially, and invited him to join in the evening repast; his cassock, saturated with rain, was taken to the fire and a cloak thrown over him instead, and the water dried from his silvery hair.

' You will like this island, I am sure,' said he ; ' it is a delightful spot—just perfection, I should call it. There is a song we sing about it ; it runs thus:

> ' " The land is fair and free.
>   The sun doth brightly shine " '——

' We've seen no sun, only rain,' growled Glum.
The priest went on :

> ' " The skies are blue, and see,
>   The silvery mountain line !
>   The sparkling waters are better than wine,
>   On no fairer land doth the sun ever shine." '

' I suppose you have never seen any other,' said Glum. ' I'll add a line, an please you :

> ' " This country is fitted only for swine." '

' To be sure, I have not seen other countries ; but I find that it is possible to be thoroughly happy

here, and that proves it not to be so very bad an
island.' The pleasant face of the priest so fully bore
out his statement that all felt cheered. 'There is
plenty to be seen here; the hills are noble with their
white hoods, like nuns in chapel, and the rivers and
lakes are full of fish. As for the people, they are
like their kin in Norway, and what better can be
said of them? Then, besides, we have a cathedral
at Skalholt, very fine, of wood and turf, and with
even glass in one window—think of that! all is very
well there, the bishop very old and a great saint,
and we have such canons for voices, all deep bass,
like trumpets.'

Thorarin turned the subject by asking whether
the rain was likely to continue through the summer.
Swerker instantly replied that there could nowhere
be a better climate than that of Iceland, there being
just sufficient rain to make the fine weather the
more enjoyable when it did come—neither cold nor
heat too intense; that the rain would blow off as
soon as the wind shifted east, and that in coming he
had seen the clouds breaking over the Oræfa.

The kindly face and voice of the priest lightened
up the whole family, like a clear ray of sun falling
through volumes of mist and slowly dispersing
them.

While the priest was talking, Glum sidled up to
his master, along the wall, and whispered hoarsely in
his ear:

'Do not fear, I will keep an eye on him;' then
slinking down to Magnus, he muttered: 'I know
that he has a dagger about him; watch that he does

not stab your father while drinking. I know what Icelanders are.'

'You have certainly chosen the best part of the island to settle in,' continued Swerker. 'If you had fixed upon the Isafiord you might have been uncomfortable, but this is the warmest and most pleasant district by far.'

'The farm came to me by inheritance through my wife,' replied Gregorius.

'The winters are terribly long here, are they not?' asked Ingibjorg.

'They are not without their pleasures,' replied the priest; 'there are sagas long and abundant enough to charm you through the dullest season, for many stirring events have happened here.'

'They must be inexhaustible,' growled Glum, 'if they relate to all the murders and house-burnings which have taken place.'

'We have a good collection of them at Skalholt,' observed Swerker; 'and during the winter, my brethren and I read them, or write others. I began last year the history of a jarl Hector, who lived out in the Greek country, or thereabouts, but I have not reached the end of it yet. If ever you come to Skalholt I will show it you: the capital letters I consider very handsome; they represent animals biting their own tails, or those of others, which is all the same. If I were to stay in this part of the island longer I might tell you quite a saga concerning the events which have occurred here, but, unfortunately, I must go back in a couple of days; to-morrow I have a very painful duty to perform.

One of our sub-deacons has run away, and set us all at defiance. I have to go after him and endeavour to bring him back. I do not like this business; I dread a repetition of the scene we had on Ascension Day; however, a duty must be performed;' and the good man sighed.

'Have you any great distance to go?' asked Gregorius.

'Hraunvellir, which is the farm I am bound for, lies round this spur of glacier; then I have to skirt Höf and Godaborg. If I could cross the glacier as the crow flies I might be there very soon, but I am too old for much climbing.'

'Let us have some sleep now,' said Gregorius, rising from his seat. 'I have caught a glimpse of clear sky through the window; if I mistake not, to-morrow will be a fine day, and we shall have plenty to do; so to rest.'

CHAPTER X.

HRAUNVELLIR.

GUDRUNA

THE following day proved clear and bright; a soft down - like cloud hung along the slopes of the ice-mountain for a little while, and then melted upward into the unbroken sky. As the good priest neared Hraunvellir, he stopped repeatedly, and conned over the address he had prepared for the wayward youth. The door was reached at last, and having tapped for admittance, he entered. Gudruna was alone in the hall; she rose proudly, and conducted Swerker to a seat of honour, and then, compressing her lips, waited till her visitor began.

'I have come from Skalholt,' said he, 'for your
son, who has left us in a very shocking manner.
His evil temper gained the mastery over him, and he
even ventured to dash aside the blessed Olaf banner,
and set us all at defiance. I hope, indeed, lady, I am
sure, that Eric must have come to a better mind by
this time ; may I see him ?'

'Go on,' Gudruna replied ; 'thy story will do as
well spoken in my ears as in his.'

'Well, lady,' said the priest, 'all I ask is, does
Eric return to us ?'

'No,' answered Gudruna, in a resolute tone.

'But consider,' urged Swerker, 'he is already in
orders, he is a sub-deacon ; he cannot cast his
orders off : a sub-deacon he must remain to the end
of his life.' Gudruna winced, and, rising from her
seat, strode up and down in deep thought. Swerker
did not speak till the lady reseated herself, then he
said quietly : 'Besides, the bishop is not likely to let
matters rest thus ; he may summon Eric and reprove
him ; should that be without avail, more serious
consequences may ensue.'

'Let me bring you some barley cake,' said
Gudruna ; 'you must be hungry.'

'Thank you, no,' answered the priest, wondering
at the change of subject.

'But you must have walked some distance,' remarked the matron, 'and it shall never be said that
my house is so inhospitable as not to provide food
for the traveller.'

'I have come from Oræfa-dal this morning,' replied Swerker.

' Indeed! exclaimed she abruptly; 'what have you been doing there?'

' The family to which it belongs have arrived, and I visited them; as being strangers, I thought——'

' Who, who?' asked Gudruna, leaning forward, her eyes lit up with a glance of eager curiosity.

' Gregorius of Thordsâ-sund,' replied Swerker.

' What!' cried a voice from behind, and instantly Eric stood before him, convulsed with excitement. ' Answer me, old man: who do you say are in Oræfa-dal now?'

' Gregorius of Thordsâ-sund,' answered the priest, gasping for breath.

The young man broke into a loud laugh, and, shaking Swerker by the hand, exclaimed: 'I thank thee for that news! Ha! didst thou ever see a rat run into the paws of the cat?' Then turning to Gudruna, he clasped her round the neck, saying: ' Mother, rejoice with me!' Dashing frantically from the door, next moment he stood shaking his hand savagely towards the white mass of the Oræfa, hissing: 'Ha, murderer! thou art come; now beware.'

Swerker in alarm left the hall, and, touching the youth on the arm, said: 'Eric, come with me to Skalholt; your old friends await you, my son, my dear son.'

The sub-deacon seemed not to heed him, but stood, his eyes fixed in the direction of Oræfa Farm, and his teeth clenched.

' All will be forgiven, Eric, only return——'

' Away,' yelled the young man, turning furiously

about, and dashing Swerker aside. 'I will never return to Skalholt; never go back to my clerkship. I have my mission to perform, and that a very unclerkly one; you shall hear of me soon.'

Swerker crossed himself, and withdrew. As he reached a lava block at some little distance from the house, he leaned against it, and, looking back, sighed: 'How strange! it seems to me as if the devil were gradually obtaining complete mastery over Eric. Yet what can have so excited him I cannot think; he meditates some ill to the household at Oræfa-dal. I shall ask for leave to stay a little longer at home, that I may watch what follows, and warn Gregorius.'

At Hraunvellir, meanwhile, mother and son were seated opposite each other, their hands clasped and their fierce eyes meeting.

'I could be a heathen,' murmured Gudruna, 'and believe that Loki had heard us call, and brought our foes within grasp.'

'Mother,' answered Eric hoarsely, 'why did Iceland ever leave its brave old gods? Mother! is there not something unchristian in these dear Northern climes, where nature herself is heathen, skies flushing with blood, earth rending herself to spout forth fire and spit out molten rock?'

'Son, son!' said Gudruna, 'think of Gregorius murdering your father and little Asmund, their dogs helping to drag them down. Eric, you will kill them too, those dogs; tear them, stamp them to death. Eric, Eric, if you fire Oræfa Farm, let Gregorius leap and dance among the flames.'

The woman rose as she spoke, working herself

into a savage excess of fury and hate. 'And, Eric, you must kill him if he shriek; and do not forget his little ones—let them writhe in the fire too.' Her voice became thick and choked; but she paced wildly before her son, and at last gasped: 'Child, give me something to break, tear, or spoil, lest I go mad with rage.'

The mother's desperate energy had overawed the son, who sat stern and self-possessed.

'Be at rest, mother,' said he; 'I shall not burn the house yet. To do so, I must take with me a sufficient number of men to surround it, that none may escape; but I intend to start at once and view the place, that I may learn the best disposition to make of my men, when I do attack it, and the number Gregorius is likely to have to assist him, should he attempt resistance.'

'And in the meanwhile I shall consume with the fire which is now burning me. Oh, Eric, be quick, as you love me!'

'Mother,' replied the young man, 'too great haste would ruin all; but trust me, revenge is as sweet to my soul as to yours.'

'Then, son, kill someone at once. I shall go myself if nothing be done. Here!' said Gudruna, throwing open a chest, and drawing forth a small blade of foreign workmanship, 'take this and feed it. Methinks, poor weapon, thou art thirsty; many a day hast thou lain in yon trunk and panted for blood. I have never drawn thee forth, dear little righter of all wrongs. My son was to have been a priest, and priests have nothing to do with thee.

Now my child is free, he will hug thee to his bosom, will feed thee soon, and slake thy thirst. Come here, Eric; look at the little sword, how it flickers with the sun shining on it! There is fire enough in its being; ay, it is like a little pointed flame, and one which cannot be quenched. There, I give it you; use it bravely.'

'Mother, how did you come by the weapon?' asked Eric, as he grasped it.

'Your father got it as a present from the King of Scotland, together with a glorious sword, the like of which is not to be seen in Iceland.'

'I know it well—I have often seen it.'

'That brave sword Onund took with him to Norway; and now, perhaps, it is hanging in the hall at Oræfa-dal. You must recover that blade, Eric; that must not be lost. Your father named it Fireheart, and this dagger Fireheart's daughter. I could tell you long stories of the deeds of that brand. How, when Snorro sent ten men by night to waylay Onund, Fireheart flew right and left, like the darts of flame in the winter sky; and how your father cut his way through the skulking thieves, and brought Fireheart dripping into the hall.'

'Now the daughter is coming to seek and to recover her father!' laughed Eric wildly.

CHAPTER XI.

Crossing the Glacier

THERE were two routes from Hraunvellir to Oræfa-dal. The one had been pursued by the priest, and was the most circuitous, as it skirted the mountain ridge which intervened between the two farms; the other tolerably direct, but toilsome, crossing the glacier in a straight line. The innate impetuosity of Eric made him take the latter. He found it, however, far less easy travelling than he had anticipated, and it was not till the afternoon that he began to descend the flank above the vale of the Oræfa. Here, in places, the rocks were so precipitous that he could only descend them with difficulty, wet as they often were with thawed ice, which trickled over beds of emerald moss, starred with the flowers of the saxifrage. Lower down, the scabious and cloudberry began to cover the patches of soil, and the descent became more easy. The young man had never been on this side of the hill before, and was consequently ignorant of the position of the farm of which he was in quest, and of the distance he had still to go. A jutting crag afforded him a station whence he could sweep the horizon with his eyes. Below him, the salient buttress of rock concealed the valley, the blue bay of Breidamark spread before him to the south-east, and to the north rose ranges of snow mountains; but no farm buildings were visible.

'The distance into the valley is not great,' said Eric, springing down a decline covered with loose pumice and lava splinters. The stones, darting from under his feet, whirled down the slant, and were followed by a sudden scream from below. The young deacon, finding he had injured someone, changed his course and descended as hastily as possible in a slanting direction. A few moments only elapsed before he had reached the dell to which the mass of loose fragments shelved, and there he found a girl, whom one of the falling stones had stunned, lying on the ground. A slight wound on the head was bleeding, and this Eric stanched, and with a little water succeeded in reviving the fainting maid. As her large, bright eyes opened and turned inquiringly upon the young man, a sudden agitation prevented

7

him from speaking. He lifted her gently on his arm;
her glossy hair broke from its bandage, and poured
over his shoulder like a stream on a rock. The girl's
eyes were unlighted with intelligence; they wandered
over the deacon's face with uncertainty as consciousness slowly returned, and she murmured 'Thorarin!'
Eric drew his face back, so that she might not see
it.

'What have you done, Thorarin?' said she slowly,
'Have you shot an arrow right through my head?'

'I have not,' faltered the youth in reply.

'I know you have,' she pursued; 'it was just like
you; I felt it shoot suddenly through me.'

'You are mistaken,' murmured Eric; 'a stone
struck you.'

'You threw it on purpose, I know,' said Ingibjorg,
for it was she, querulously.

'You are wounded, but only slightly,' replied the
deacon, 'and I have washed the place; it will soon
heal.'

The girl, who had by this time thoroughly regained
her senses, turned her head sharply round, for the
voice struck her as not belonging to her brother;
and, seeing the flushed face of the stranger bent
over her, she started to her feet in amazement, and
stood, her brow tinged with red, meditating some
indignant speech, when Eric dropped on one knee,
caught her hand between his own, and, looking
earnestly up in her face, said, 'Dear lady, believe
me, I never intended to injure you. I ask your
pardon, and will do whatever you may choose to bid
me, to testify my sorrow.'

The handsome, pleading countenance before her overcame all Ingibjorg's resentment, and, turning her face aside with pouting lips, she gave the desired forgiveness.

' Fair mountain flower,' said he in the peculiarly soft voice he possessed when not speaking under the influence of violent passion, ' how could you venture into such wild solitudes as these ?'

' I dislike sitting at home all day, and especially on a day which is really at times bright. I cannot spin, or pickle cranberries when the sun is shining : I like to enjoy myself a little, before the frightful winter sets in.'

' Frightful winter !' exclaimed Eric; ' why, it is the best part of the year.'

' A charming part of the year, certainly, when one has to shiver for eight months, without once stopping; eating nothing but leathery, wind-dried fish, and cold meat pickled in whey. I am sure it is a marvel that people manage to live all that while without choking themselves with the fish-bones, or being made ill with the sour meat. Then, there is no sun to speak of.'

' But there are enjoyments which amply make up for all of which we are deprived.'

' Well, that may be,' retorted Ingibjorg; ' we poor women get less to do, that is one comfort. In summer we are worked like common churls, what with hay-making, pickling, and the like. Just look how freckled I am—which comes of tossing the grass about this morning. I shall go home now,' added Ingibjorg, taking a few steps forward.

'Not alone!' exclaimed Eric, springing after her.
'You cannot walk without support; lean on me.'

The girl, whose steps really faltered, was obliged to
comply, and the young man conducted her gently
in the direction she required.

'But,' said she hesitatingly, 'I am troubling you,
kind stranger.'

'Surely,' replied the youth, 'since it is by my fault
that you are hurt, I am bound to conduct you safely
home.'

'I dare say when I get home,' said the girl, 'father
will not notice my being hurt, and as for Thorarin,
he will laugh at me about it.'

'Who is Thorarin?' asked Eric, his cheeks flushing. 'His was the first name you uttered on returning to your senses; is he——' He bit his lip to
prevent it from quivering.

'Dear Thorarin!' murmured Ingibjorg. 'Next to
my father, there is no one I love better on earth.'

Eric trembled; his face became scarlet. Ingibjorg
turned her eyes towards him, and noticing the effect
of her words, maliciously proceeded:

'But that is not to be wondered at, for I think
he loves me as much as I do him.'

'Who is he?' said Eric huskily, and with
emotion.

'Thorarin?' exclaimed the girl. 'He is only a few
years older than I am. You are standing still;
perhaps I can walk alone now.'

'Tell me, dear mountain flower,' entreated Eric
with vehemence, 'tell me who this Thorarin is.'

Ingibjorg looked on the young man, and inwardly

rejoiced at the conquest before she replied composedly, 'Why, my brother, to be sure.'

'Oh, your brother!' Eric uttered a sigh of relief.

As the two descended the hill, they talked pleasantly together. The distance was not great, but the girl could not walk fast. As Oræfa-dal Farm came in sight, nestling below the flank of the hill, Ingibjorg paused by a rock, from beneath which bubbled up a spring of sparkling water.

'This is the place whence we get water. See, here is my pitcher. I came to fill it a while ago, but wandered on among the rocks for a little novelty.'

'And that is your home,' said Eric, pointing to the farm. 'Here we must part.'

The girl held out her hand, and bade him farewell, giving him a kindly glance out of her clear, deep eyes. The youth's handsome face had impressed her, and the uncontrolled admiration he evinced towards her flattered her vain heart, at the same time that the suddenness of this affection somewhat startled her.

'Before we part,' said she, 'tell me what your name is.'

'My name is Eric,' answered the youth. 'I am well born, and of no mean position in this island; but, pretty flower, shall we never meet again? I must, I will see you often.'

'That is possible enough,' replied Ingibjorg. 'Perhaps you live near Oræfa-dal.'

'Oræfa-dal!' exclaimed the sub-deacon, almost with a shriek. 'Where is that?'

'You see it before you,' replied Ingibjorg, pointing to the farm.

Eric staggered back against a fragment of rock.

'And you ?'

'I am the daughter of Sira Gregorius, the owner of the valley,' answered the girl, raising herself proudly.

The young man's face became livid : his hands dropped as if paralyzed at his side. He fixed his eyes on the maiden with an earnestness which made her start.

'Farewell,' said she, retiring.

Eric remained motionless, looking with the same intense expression after her. She took but a few steps, and then, turning her face, waved her hand towards him. He started from his lethargy, darted after her, caught the fingers, and said between his teeth :

'Flower, shall I see you again?'

'How can I tell,' asked Ingibjorg.

'Do you come often to this well for water ?' he inquired.

'Every morning and evening,' was the reply. 'Why do you want to know ?'

'Dear mountain flower!' murmured Eric, pressing her hand to his lips.

Ingibjorg snatched it away, blushed, and ran hastily down the slope, without once looking round ; but Eric remained bereft of motion, kneeling and gazing with a wild, undecided stare at Oræfa-dal Farm.

What was passing in his mind the reader may well guess. The promise to his mother, his own determination to avenge his father; and, on the other side, this new passion, which he felt he could not, would not try to overcome. Time passed, and he was still kneeling in the same spot, the struggle still raging in his breast.

CHAPTER XII.

Eric Lying in Wait

GREGORIUS and his brother were pacing up and down before the wood-rick at the back of their house, while G l u m heaped up and arranged the bundles which h a d b e e n brought in during that and the preceding day.

It was evening, and the tender sunlight suffused the broad back of the Oræfa mountain in gold and rose tint. A sunk fence divided the patch of land on which the farm was erected from the common-land which rose behind, and served to carry off the water which descended from the hill. In this lurked Eric, close to the two brothers, yet unseen.

'Rolf,' said the elder brother, 'I have several plans for improving the farm. There is that waste land by the river; surely it might be enclosed, and made into good pasture.'

'It is flooded occasionally,' observed Rolf, 'and the ash which is swept from under the glacier checks the growth of grass for years. I doubt the expediency of walling it round, when a sudden rise in the flood might overthrow the erection in a night.'

'Well, what do you say to a ditch about it? That would carry off a good deal of the surface water.'

'There are other matters to be attended to before we can dig trenches,' said Rolf. 'We have not as yet a proper fold for the sheep during the winter. I must see about the construction of one as soon as any hands can be spared from things of earlier importance.'

'There will certainly be a great deal to be done this season. We must have additional fishing-boats,' said Gregorius. 'But whom have we here?'

A strange lad came towards Gregorius.

'I am sent from the priest Swerker,' said he. 'He bids you God-speed, and prays that you will send one of your sons or your brother to see him to-morrow evening, as he would say something of importance to him. He cannot come himself, as he is wearied with his long walk to Hraunvellir. His mother's cottage stands on the east bank of the White River, on the Breidamark sands.'

'Thank the pious father from me,' answered the
bonder, 'and tell him that my son Magnus shall be
with him at an hour before sundown to-morrow.
Now, my lad, go within, and the servants will supply
thee with refreshment.'

Glum had turned his head on hearing a strange
voice. As he did so, his keen eye rested for a
moment on the moat. He might have seen something, for a look of animation, a glow of cheerful-
ness, suddenly lighted up his previously downcast
features. First slowly knotting a cord which kept
the bundles in place, he then walked deliberately to
the farther side of the stack, and was necessarily out
of sight.

'I suppose, Rolf, you hardly care to go to the
priest the ensuing evening? There will be so much
to be done that you cannot well be spared; and,
moreover, the old man can have nothing of real
consequence to communicate.'

'Magnus will do just as well,' answered Rolf.

'Glum, Glum, where are you?' called Gregorius.
'Take this lad within, and see that he be attended
to. Whither has the fellow gone?'

'Gone after some withes, no doubt,' answered
Rolf. 'Here, lad, turn the corner of the house, and
enter the large door.'

The boy went off; meanwhile, a dagger was un-
sheathed at a couple of steps from the brothers.

The writer feels some hesitation in pursuing his
narrative. Not that he fears his characters and
their actions may appear in other colouring than
that which represents the real state of Icelandic

society in the fourteenth century, for he believes
that there is authority for his minutest details. The
real ground of fear with him is, that the terrible
features of those times may prove repulsive to his
readers; and yet, if he would be consistent with the
spirit of the age which he delineates, many scenes
of blood and outbursts of savage rage must appear
prominently in his story. Every nation in its child-
hood began to play with edged tools, but none with
greater boldness than the Scandinavian. Whether
these stormy passions have wholly spent themselves, or are brooding still over our horizon, it is
not for the author to say; whether the ferocity in
our nature has at all showed itself of late among
our countrymen—whether, for instance, our gilded
leopards have contented themselves with catching
mice, or, again, whether the love of excitement,
which nowadays quenches itself in a novel, instead
of driving men to deeds of heroism, be more whole-
some than its first development—are points which
must be left to his readers to determine. However,
he ventures to say that if the features of mediæval
society be looked at with naked eye, and not through
nineteenth-century spectacles, marvellous reality and
truth will be seen, such as is not common in these
times. The Middle Ages were times presenting
violent contrasts. With blood-smirched hands, in
the glare of blazing homesteads, notable deeds of
mercy, self-devotion, or valour were performed.
Then brightness was dashed into the darkness. If
there were keen winds and chill showers, the buds of
many flowers burst open in the May of civilization;

and those leaflets which appeared were full of the life of warm gales and soft dews. Now we have lost the frosts and winds, and rejoice in our autumn, with its smell of corruption, and its leaves pulled from the branches and strewed for us to trample on, or to scrape together or anatomize.

The Middle Ages were times of honesty and earnestness. What was to be done, good or evil, was done with all man's might; and from the actions, even though of blood, bright sparks of courage and true-heartedness were elicited. Perhaps we may have gained prudence and justice, but we may have lost the equally cardinal virtues, temperance and fortitude. The present age is one of indifference, and the men of this generation lie under an evenly-graduated sky of gray, wrapt in themselves alone. There was great freshness and reality in the old days, with their long stalking shadows and bright kindling gleams of sun.

In the meanwhile Eric stole up the bank; the brothers had their faces turned from him. The dagger flickered in the bad sub-deacon's hand.

'Poor Norway!' sighed Gregorius. 'I wonder whether we shall see the pine-girt fiords again.'

Rolf shook his head.

'It makes me sad to think of Thordsâ-sund, and all the happy days spent there,' said he.

There was a pause. Eric stood like an icicle, holding his breath.

At last Gregorius said, in a quiet tone: 'Brother, does it not show how good God is in providing this home for us. Little did I value or care for this

IN ANOTHER MOMENT GLUM HAD DASHED HIM TO THE GROUND.

inheritance ; indeed, I often wished to sell it, but it was not left me without purpose. I suppose the smallest events of life are in reality very solemn and important, and hereafter we shall see that little things we have slighted here have been——'

There was a rush, a cry of astonishment from Rolf. Eric had sprung on him with his uplifted dagger. The blow would have fallen, had not a powerful hand almost instantaneously grasped the youth's arm, and in another moment Glum had dashed him to the ground. This was the first time, since he had been in the family, that the pilot was heard to laugh.

Almost before the brothers had recovered from their surprise, Glum had carried off the culprit, and fastened him into the fish-house, from which he knew escape was impossible.

CHAPTER XIII.

ESCAPED.

'WHO can he be?' asked Rolf of his brother, as the three men seated themselves by the fire in the hall.

'A madman, I should suppose,' answered Gregorius.

'Not a bit of it,' exclaimed Glum. 'These young Icelanders are all of a piece, equally wild, headstrong, bloodthirsty. However, this one is safe for sometime to come. Speak the word, and I'll cut his throat.'

'Why, father, what is the matter?' asked Ingibjorg, stepping forward from a corner where she had been engaged. 'Of what young Icelander are you talking?'

'Never mind, daughter; it nothing concerns you.'

'You had better go out, and see that the maidens have milked the cows,' said Rolf.

When Ingibjorg hesitated, her father peremptorily said:

'Go, daughter.'

'I wonder about what young man they are talking,' mused she on leaving the room with a very ill grace. 'And I should like to know what he has been doing to call down their anger. He must be a born Icelander, for Glum said as much, so he cannot be one of my father's folk. Who can he possibly be? And Glum wants to cut his throat, does he?—cut a young man's throat! Perhaps he may be a nice young man, perhaps good-looking. I should not be surprised if they have fallen upon that handsome stranger, who was so very courteous to me the day before yesterday, and came to see me again at the well these two mornings. If it be, then Glum shall never touch a hair of his head. I dare say the poor fellow has been speaking to my father and uncle about me. He seems such a simple, earnest-hearted youth, and—he is so very good-looking. Perhaps they have shut him up somewhere. My father fancies him a madman, just because he has an affection for me! That is like father! Mad because he admires me. Then, I know what will be the end of it. Thorarin will come in, Glum will tell him all, with a great deal more that is utterly untrue, and they will just go and put an end to my dear friend.'

8

Ingibjorg became vehement, and paced the grass with hasty steps.

'Where can they have confined him?' she thought. 'There is the fish-house; I wonder whether he is shut into that? I can but find out.'

At once she broke into a low, plaintive song, and walked slowly to the place. Then, leaning against the door-post, she continued to warble her tender Norse melody.

'Dear flower,' said a voice from within, 'are you here?'

'Why, what brings you into this place?' Ingibjorg asked, partly with feigned, partly with real astonishment.

Eric hesitated.

'Open the door, pretty one, and I will tell you.'

'You will promise me not to escape without my leave?' she said.

'Yes, I promise.'

In a moment the large bolt was slid back, and Ingibjorg half opened the valve.

Eric took her hand; the girl blushed a little, ashamed at what she had done, and afraid of her father's anger.

'They were too hasty with you, friend,' she murmured. 'They had no right to put you in here.'

'Have they told you their story?' asked the youth.

'No, not entirely, but I guessed,' answered Ingibjorg. 'Glum shall not hurt you, although he wished to cut your throat, and would have done so had my father suffered it'

Eric's brow darkened.

' I have no doubt he did. Your father, dear bird, has fearfully injured me.'

' But I never intended to—I have had no hand in this,' faltered Ingibjorg; and her little heart fluttered. ' You know I would not hurt you.'

Eric pressed her hand.

' May I go ?' he asked. ' I remain a prisoner to you.'

' Go,' said the girl, throwing the door open.

Eric darted past ; but as he ran along the turf his eye caught sight of the fallen dagger. He stooped, picked it up, and in another moment was beyond the moat and among the lava crags.

Ingibjorg went quietly back into the hall, and seated herself at her work. The men on her entry changed their subject of conversation to matters of ordinary interest, Gregorius wishing the danger in which Rolf had been to be concealed from his daughter, lest it should cause her uneasiness and alarm.

It was not until late in the evening that the escape of the prisoner was discovered by Glum, who had gone to the fish-house to carry the captive something to eat, and bring him before Gregorius, who had determined on examining into the cause of the assault.

On finding the door open, Glum returned to the hall with a more than usually ominous look. He sidled up to his master, and having seated himself, began quietly to warm his hands.

Gregorius, seeing that something had gone wrong, inquired in a low voice what it was.

'Nothing,' replied Glum, with a shrug of the shoulders.

'Is he safe ?'

'Quite,' answered the pilot, with a short laugh. 'He is off.'

Gregorius looked distressed.

'How did that occur ?' he asked.

'I'll tell you my opinion,' said the pilot, pursing his lips. 'There is a gang of these cut-throat rascals prowling among the hills. It was no great matter for them to let one of their comrades out when shut into a block-house with no one to look after him.'

'What is there gone wrong ?' questioned Ingibjorg.

'Nothing concerning you,' answered Rolf.

Glum stole out of the house, and waited till Thorarin came up from fishing. He narrated the whole occurrence to him, and the young man, firing with excitement, spent the night with Glum in searching the mountain side for traces of the assailant. The night was as bright as the day. There was no darkness, and they overran the neighbourhood for some hours. Nothing was, however, to be found, for Eric was already far across the glacier, and nearing his mother's home.

When the young man entered Hraunvellir, Gudruna sprang to meet him, but no embrace did she vouchsafe till she had drawn Fireheart's sister from his bosom.

'So there is nothing done, after all!' she exclaimed, stamping her feet and throwing the dagger across the hall. 'And you promised me, son——'

'Mother,' answered the youth, 'I did what I could. That little sword would have been fleshed had I not been captured, and it is only by chance that I have escaped.'

'Wherefore did they capture you?'

'I sprang on one of our enemies, Gregorius or his brother, I know not which, and would have struck him down, had not one of the farm men withheld my hand, thrown me down, and, with the help of the others, fastened me into an outhouse.'

'Then, how didst thou escape?'

Eric reddened and hung his head. With difficulty he stammered:

'The daughter let me go free. I love her, mother.'

Gudruna paced to and fro with vehemence, her lips compressed. She did not say a word.

'Mother,' continued Eric, 'there is hope yet. To-day the bonder's son goes to visit the priest Swerker, who intends to warn him of his danger. Give me two men, as the fellow is not likely to go alone, and he shall never see Oræfa-dal again.'

Gudruna waved her hand impatiently.

'Well, mother,' said the young man, 'will that satisfy you?'

'No!' burst forth the angry woman. 'Out of my sight till you have fulfilled your promise!'

Eric stepped across the hall to pick up Fireheart's sister.

'Leave that!' shouted Gudruna; then she added with a low rattling laugh, 'I retain that for a separate office.'

Eric strode out of the hall.

CHAPTER XIV.

AN EVENING WITH FATHER SWERKER.

Thorarin & Magnus at the ford

THE following evening was wild and tempestuous; the dark rack, ragged and threatening, came up with the wind at sun-down, blotting the tender gray of the firmament with masses of whirling brown vapour. The last lights flickering along the hills showed them like fuming ash-heaps, and then smeared them over with a falling veil of iron-gray. The sea thundered over the Breidamark bar. Throughout the night its white line of lashing, plunging foam was visible, the shore vibrating beneath the strokes; the White River raved, whirled and battled with the moving mounds of brine, its short waves recoiling and swept on again.

Swerker's cottage was not far from the mouth of the river, perched on a rock which trembled with the blows of the surge, and its inmates trembled too. No rain had fallen, but the wind poured relentlessly in from the sea, carrying specks of foam upon its wings.

A bright fire was blazing in the cottage, and a large oil-lamp swung pendent from the roof. In the seat of honour sat the good priest's mother, a worthy aged soul, very deaf, rather blind, but with a warm, fresh heart, occupied almost entirely by her gray-haired son.

By his own wish Thorarin had accompanied Magnus. The priest was in the highest spirits; he apologized for his humble fare, yet with full consciousness of the excellency of his meal, and delicacy of the curd, flavoured with cranberry.

'Did you find any difficulty in fording the White River? Is it all swollen?' asked the priest.

'As usual, I suppose,' replied Magnus; 'but we did not ford it. Thorarin has a boat; we crossed in that, though not without some difficulty; the stream is very turbulent.'

'If it were a quiet lake there would be no sport in passing,' said Thorarin. 'If a thing is to be done, let it be battled through: then it gains value. Had there been a smooth path or slide between Oræfa-dal and this house I should not have come.'

'I remember that river so full that it swept the wall of your farm enclosure,' observed Swerker. 'It rose in one night, and at daybreak the sea was black, and encumbered with ice for a great distance from shore.'

'How came that about?' asked Magnus.

'There had been tremblings in the Oræfa for a month, but nothing of importance took place until the night I tell you of, when the water suddenly burst forth from the roots of the glacier in a huge torrent. The weather was perfectly calm, and the sky clear, so that during the day the mountain was visible, enveloped in a dense cloud of steam, from which repeated explosions and shocks were heard, which sufficiently alarmed all who dwelt in the neighbourhood. I removed my mother to a securer spot, but in a week the steam-fog blew off, the river sank, and all returned to its wonted tranquillity. We saw then that a portion of the glacier had fallen in; the rock beneath, having become heated with the subterraneous fires, had melted the nether ice; while the upper, left without support, had crushed inwards.'

'Was there no eruption?' asked Magnus.

'None,' answered the father. 'There has been no outburst from the Oræfa for a long while; but there was one sorely disastrous within my recollection, from Kötlugia. I was quite a little boy then, but I well remember the redness of the sky in that direction, the shuddering of the ground, and the frenzy of the tides which, on a calm day, rose and tumbled about these rocks. Whole districts were submerged in bubbling black mud, sheets of blazing lava poured from mouths which gaped in

the mountain's side and fell over the precipices
in heavy burning masses. The cones on the mountain-top continued the whole while roaring, and
blowing up live cinders or jets of mingled fire and
steam.'

'I should like to see an eruption of the Oræfa!'
exclaimed Thorarin.

'Should you?' asked Father Swerker incredu-
lously. 'Should you wish to see your home broken
up and tossed down a stream of hot mud like a
bundle of crumpled straw?'

'I heard strange sounds yesterday while lying on
a rock; they were as though coming from under-
ground, such as I never noticed in Norway. I
heard a muttering, then a low rattle as if stones
were being rolled down an incline; but I attributed
that to the dwergir or Trolls mineral-hunting,' remarked Thorarin.

'Such noises are not uncommon,' said the old
man. 'When one has lived long near the foot of a
volcano, one becomes so used to them as hardly
to notice their recurrence.'

'My father has been proposing to enclose the low
land by the water's edge; if those floods you spoke
of are frequent, his labour will be wasted,' said
Magnus.

'Let him not think again of doing so,' advised
the priest. 'These glacier streams, which run for
such a brief course, are most uncertain, and the less
their banks are meddled with the better; they are
affected by the temperature, by the volcanic fires in
the mountain, and by the tides, which will some-

times raise a bore which will run far up the river, a huge upper wave of salt water, while a stream of fresh is flowing beneath in an opposite direction.'

' By the way, there are other dangers incidental to a residence here besides volcanoes,' observed Magnus.

' To what do you allude ?' inquired the priest. ' I was about to forewarn you of one myself.'

Suddenly the dog, which had been crouching at Thorarin's feet, rose, snuffed around him and howled.

' Let all good spirits bless the Lord,' muttered Swerker's aged mother in her high seat.

' Keep the hound quiet, brother,' begged Magnus; ' you need not have brought it with you.' Then, turning towards the father, he continued : ' The danger I mean is the dagger of a secret enemy. Yesterday a young man sprang on my Uncle Rolf, and would undoubtedly have killed him had not our pilot, Glum, been watching the fellow, and ready at the moment to prevent him. What is the matter with that dog ?'

The animal was erect, its nose forward, and its white fangs showing, while a preparatory growl rattled in its throat. Swerker drove a stake into the fire, and a volume of ruddy spark and flame flashed upward.

' By Thor's hammer!' exclaimed Thorarin, starting to his feet; both he and Magnus caught a momentary glance of a face, lighted with the scarlet of the glowing embers, gleaming in at the small square window.

Thorarin bounded to the door, swung it open, and

ran out. For a moment he saw a dark form cutting the horizon, and then it vanished; he hurried after it, but could see nothing further in the iron-gray fog. On his return to the cottage he found Swerker sitting with the greatest composure by the fire. The old man bade him close the door, and then, with a grave smile, said:

'You need not be alarmed; that visitor, I suspect, was only a poor sailor who has been drowned in this fearful storm. We in Iceland think it a good omen when a disembodied spirit steals in and seats himself at our firesides. Had you not scared him away, doubtless that chair, which you may perceive is left vacant, would be occupied.'

'What!' exclaimed Thorarin with a laugh, 'have I been running after a ghost?'

'Heaven knows,' answered Swerker. 'This, I can assure you, that after death relations often re-visit their families on jovial occasions. There are instances of common occurrence when the spirits of fathers or mothers have seated themselves at their children's marriage supper board.'

'But——' began Magnus.

'This apparition, I doubt not, was not one of these,' interrupted the priest. 'More likely it was a drowned fisherman. There was a family* in the north by Snaefel who were seated once at their evening meal. It was such a time as this; their conversation was running fast and joyous, when— the door opened and six men entered, water stream-ing from their clothes. They said not a word, but

* This story is related in the Eyrbyggia Saga.

placed themselves before the fire; the astonished
family saw the moisture stream from their dresses,
but without the sealskin clothes becoming a whit
more dry; the fire flared on the gray faces, but
without kindling a glow of warmth in the ashen
cheeks. Before morning these men were gone.
That night, at the same watch as that on which
these spectres had appeared, a fishing-smack with
six sailors had been lost off the coast.'

'God grant rest to the souls of all faithful de-
parted!' murmured the priest's mother, crossing her
hands on her breast.

'There is a fearful story of Thorir Bægfôt,' said
Swerker, 'who after death struggled with and
strangled people at the doors of their houses; but
I shall not tell you of him now, but reserve his
saga for some future occasion. Now, my children,
I have another matter about which to speak to you.
You tell me that an assault has already been made
on your uncle's person; tell me, has the assailant
escaped?'

'He has,' replied Magnus. 'The door of the shed
in which he was confined has been opened, and he
allowed to escape.'

'I have seen enough to convince me that your
father is an object of abhorrence to the family at
Hraunvellir, a place you may not have heard of, but
situated at no vast distance from you. What has
caused this animosity I do not know, perhaps you
may; but I am sure that both mother and son are
burning to revenge themselves on you for some
injury, real or imaginary. You have told me that

a first blow has been struck. I warn you—repeat my words to your father—I warn you to be on your guard, for your enemies are powerful and unscrupulous.'

'I shall go and burn Hraunvellir down to-morrow night,' observed Thorarin with considerable satisfaction. 'I am thankful to you, good father, for having told me who the foe is with whom I am to engage.'

'For heaven's sake!' exclaimed the priest, 'hold from such rashness. Keep on the watch, and you may summon Eric before the Thing; but if you take the law into your own hands you are sure to suffer.'

'Law!' burst forth contemptuously from Thorarin's lips; 'as if I should think of law for one moment. Give me my good sword and a practised enemy before my face, and all our little quarrels shall be settled in an hour.'

'Brother,' said Magnus, 'you must on no account move until you have consulted with father, Rolf, and Glum.'

'No, that I shall not,' answered the impetuous youth; 'for I shall want hands if the little work at Hraunvellir is to be accomplished satisfactorily.'

'You shall not do this,' said the priest.

'We shall see what my father advises,' said Magnus. 'Now I think we must be going; the wind has slightly abated.'

'Farewell, then, good host,' Thorarin said, clasping the old man's hand; and then, with a courteous salutation to the aged mother, he stepped forth into the storm.

Magnus followed more leisurely, and the two walked in the direction of their landing place.

'I am glad we have brought the boat,' said Magnus. 'A wade through the stream of hardly-dissolved snow would not be agreeable, even were it feasible.'

'Yonder is the ford, below those rocks; we keep along the high ground up the river.'

'What are you doing with your belt?' asked Magnus.

'Getting my sword ready, brother,' answered Thorarin in a low voice; 'for, to tell you truly, that face which looked in at the window was more like that of a living man than of a spectre. I should not be surprised if we were waylaid; the dog, you see, is uneasy, snuffing at some scent on the ground. Ha! he points towards the ford; it is almost a pity that we do not go that way.'

'You may rely upon it there is no one waylaying us,' said Magnus, laughing. 'Who was to know that we were coming to the priest's to-night?'

'I forgot that,' responded Thorarin with a sigh of disappointment; 'come, let us on quicker.'

CHAPTER XV.

THE FORD.

RIC and two farm-men were stationed by the river-side.

'You are sure that this is the only ford?' asked the youth, 'for I would not miss them, now that we have come so far.'

'There is none other,' answered the man addressed; 'this is the only place where they can possibly pass, and this is bad enough.'

'There were two only, Olver?' asked the subdeacon.

'Two and a dog,' was the reply. 'I looked in at the window, and saw an old man and woman——'

'Yes, yes,' interrupted Eric—'the priest and his mother.'

'Besides these were a couple of young men. The dog scented me, and began to growl.'

' When they come upon us, it will be suddenly,'
observed the other man; 'we shall have no chance
of hearing them nor of seeing them approach, on
account of this storm. The rain drives, and the wind
roars—to blind and deafen.'

' I wish the hut were visible from hence,' said
Eric.

' Were it not better to go nearer ?' asked Olver.

' No,' answered the youth. ' The noise of fighting
would infallibly call out the priest and his two men-
servants; the old man has a powerful arm.'

' I do not believe he has any men in the house,'
said one of the men.

' There are,' answered Eric sharply. ' I have
heard him, at Skalholt, talk enough about them and
their powers of net-drawing.'

' I know that there are,' added Olver, ' for when I
walked round the cottage I saw tokens enough of
man's work, and the priest does not live there.'

' They are spending a long time with the graybeard,'
said Eric. ' Wielund, have you a sword as well as
Olver ?'

' A sharp one of my father's,' answered the
fellow.'

' Hold !' exclaimed Olver, ' I thought I saw some
figure on the ridge.'

Eric looked up the slope, but the darkness was so
dense, and the glimpse of clear sky, against which
the men for whom they were watching might
have been revealed, so momentarily blurred over
with a whirl of gray rack, that he strained his eyes
in vain.

'Stand firm and be ready,' he muttered between his teeth, drawing his sword at the same moment.

Some time passed, and no further intimation of anyone's approach was given.

'I believe that I saw them,' whispered Olver. 'They must have missed the turning to the ford, and have gone too far up the river; never mind, they will return directly.'

'They may have a boat,' remarked Wielund.

'I never thought of that !' exclaimed Eric. ' Run, Olver — run up the hill and follow the ridge; Wielund, go to the priest's house and see if they are gone. I shall keep watch here lest they should have overshot the mark, and return this way to the ford.'

The men started, and the young man paced excitedly by the edge of the stream, his sword in hand.

The river at this point was broad and shallow; in some places, however, where large boulders blocked the course, the water whirled past with velocity, and formed channels of considerable depth between the rocks. In many places the passenger had to wade to his armpits. By day the ford was only to be attempted with caution; and by night, to traverse the river by the ford was necessarily attended with considerable danger. The opposite shore was hardly visible.

'If they escape me,' mused the young man, 'how can I face my mother; what could I say to her ? I wish that I had that dagger here; it would be a more serviceable weapon than this broad, ponderous

9

sword. Why would not my mother let me take it again ? What could she want with it ? She had a separate office it was to fulfil; I should like very much to know what she meant by that. How she looked, too, when I spoke about pretty Ingibjorg! I thought she would have struck me dead, and yet she never uttered a word!'

Eric paced more rapidly to and fro. 'Why not let me take that little dagger ? She does not intend——' His flesh shivered, and his blood curdled in his veins.

At that moment there was a laugh, and an exclamation from the river.

'Be careful, Magnus; we shall be swept into the sea!'

Eric started. The voice said again hastily, 'Mind your oar! we are at the ford; back, bring her head round!'

The sub-deacon muttered a curse and sprang into the water. It rose at once to his middle; when he had crossed before, it had reached his knees. Olver ran up at the same moment. 'The river is swollen, and is rising still,' he whispered; 'you cannot venture.'

'I must,' said Eric savagely; 'they shall not escape like this;' and he pressed on. Olver lifted a stone and put it on his own head, and then stepped in also—but not to cross. The stream swept past with such velocity that Eric lost his footing; Olver caught him, and only with difficulty brought him to the bank.

'Make her head fast!' called Thorarin on the other side.

'Safe now,' answered Magnus ; 'jump out.'

With rage Eric cut at the bushes and the grass. Wielund came up, and the three conversed in a low voice, for they thought it not right to let those who had escaped know of their late peril.

'Well,' said Olver with a laugh, 'you escaped from them, and now they have played you the same turn.'

'We shall be able to cross by daylight,' observed Wielund ; 'if we can find no footing, we must swim.'

'If they had not escaped us!' muttered Eric wrathfully. 'We made a mistake. We ought to have set fire to the priest's house while we were sure of having them ; a bird in hand is worth two in a wood.'

'After all,' said Wielund, 'they escaped our hands but to fall into your mother's.'

'What do you mean ?' asked the sub-deacon sharply.

'Nothing, but that the party lady Gudruna has sent are likely enough to capture these two.'

Eric dashed his sword furiously against the sand and stones. 'What party has she sent?'

Wielund did not answer at once ; he seemed surprised. 'That which she has ordered to Oræfa-dal ; surely she intended that you should meet those who have just escaped, so as to prevent them from rendering aid while the farm was being attacked.'

'I never heard anything of this,' said Eric, with agitation. 'How know you of it ?'

'When I returned for my sword, I heard Thorstein the Fox ordering two of the men to accompany him to Oræfa-dal, and to take their weapons with them.'

'Only three!' exclaimed the young man. 'Then she could not intend them to assault the farm. Why did you not tell me of this before?'

'I thought your expedition and that of your mother were planned in concert,' answered Wielund. 'I know that Thorstein was to carry off a woman from the farm, as I heard him complain that in consequence he would have to make the circuit of the hills on his way back.'

'A woman!' almost shrieked Eric, standing suddenly still. 'From Oræfa-dal?—to bring her to my mother!' He stood trembling with excitement; then, with 'Follow me, my friends!' he plunged into the river and battled furiously with the waves.

Olver and Wielund looked uncertainly at each other for one moment, then fixed their eyes on the opposite bank—the morning was already breaking, for in early autumn nights are short in the North. Drawing a deep breath, the two men rushed in.

ARLY on the following morning, before the family had separated for the day, and just as they had terminated their morning meal, a stranger stepped into the hall. Gregorius instantly rose to offer the visitor a seat at the board, which the man accepted, and ate plentifully of what was placed before him, having previously laid a small bundle he had brought with him on a bench near the door. Icelandic etiquette forbade Gregorius to inquire the object of this visit, and he waited patiently until the stranger should choose to reveal something connected with himself. While he was eating, however, the family had a good opportunity for examining the man's countenance. This was not attractive; a large amount of red hair covered the greater part of it. His eyes were bright, keen, and continually in motion—at one time scanning his food, at another

those who sat at table, or wandering round the hall.
The features were, as far as discernible, inexpres-
sive, only once, as the eyes lighted on Magnus'
sword, which hung against the wall, kindling into a
strange smile, passing off into a scowl, and almost
instantaneously lost in dull stolidity.

'It was a fierce night,' said Gregorius; 'the
clouds broke over the Oræfa, and this morning our
river is swollen so as to cover the water-meadows.'

'It nearly carried Thorarin and me into the sea,'
said Magnus. 'We had hard work, I can assure
you, to bring our boat to shore.'

'It is well you did not attempt the ford,' said the
father.

'The night was a bad one,' growled the visitor.
'I was out in it all.'

'Little rain fell, except among the mountains,'
observed the bonder.

'I came over the mountains,' said the red-haired
man, leaning back, for he had eaten and drunk as
much as he wanted, 'I am come from Raudaberg.
Sira Bjarni Elidagrimson sent me to you with a
little present; he claims relationship to you through
your mother. My name is Thorstein the Fox. I
always tell my name wherever I go that it may be
remembered. I am called the Fox because I am
red, though, indeed, here in Iceland, the foxes are
blue in summer and white in winter. Elsewhere, I
am told, foxes are red. But I care not; the fox is
the most sagacious of animals.' He rose abruptly,
and, fetching his bundle, opened it and displayed a
horn set with silver, and a mantle-clasp.

Ingibjorg exclaimed with delight, but her father and brothers showed a becoming gravity.

Thorstein allowed the presents to be well examined, and then he said with the air of one who was repeating a lesson or message by heart: 'My master sends you, by me, a kindly greeting. He desires that continual love may bind his family to yours, and that when you meet him your hand may be ready to grasp his; that you will be prepared to lend him the assistance of your voice at the Thing or your sword in a fray, as his will ever be ready on your behalf. My master Bjarni of Raudaberg is the son of Elidagrim, whose father was Thorer, who married Aud, the daughter of Olver-Frode, whose brother was Eystein, and their father Alf——'

'Alf had but one son,' said Glum, fixing his cold gray eye on the stranger.

'He had two, by the holy Thorlak!' exclaimed Thorstein. 'Alf, by his wife Sigunna, had two sons, Olver and Eystein, from whom thy wife, Master Gregorius, is descended.'

'Alf had but one son, and that was Eystein,' persisted Glum. 'Come outside the door and I will convince you with my sword.'

'Forbear,' said Gregorius angrily; 'I will have no fighting on such a trifle, Glum. If Bjarni of Raudaberg be willing to consider himself our relation and friend, I am willing to grasp his hand, even should the connection be somewhat doubtful.'

'I have known and repeated the genealogy long enough to be certain,' said Glum doggedly. 'Eystein was Alf's only son.'

'Be silent,' commanded Gregorius.

The pilot retreated to the door, with threatening looks directed upon Thorstein, who seemed disposed to receive them with sulky contempt. Glum stationed himself by the entrance, and, taking up a net, began to fasten the weights where they were loose.

'You must remain here awhile and rest,' said the bonder to the messenger. 'To-morrow morning you shall return to your master with a suitable answer. Raudaberg is surely at no trifling distance hence, for I do not remember to have heard the name.'

'That may well be,' remarked Thorstein, 'for it is beyond the Lomagnupr headland. I have had a long day and night journey, and, moreover, have injured my leg.'

'I noticed that you walked lame,' said Gregorius.

'Mine was a road by which one cannot take a horse,' growled the Fox; 'for there are water and glacier to cross, unless one goes a vast way round. I rode as far as I could.'

Glum worked restlessly at his net, occasionally muttering to himself. His master saw that he was not to be safely left about the house so long as the guest was present, and he determined on getting rid of him for the day.

'Friend,' said he to his guest, 'my sons and I must leave you now. Ingibjorg, see that Bjarni's messenger lacks nothing. I would advise him to sleep by the fire; but see, daughter, that he be well attended to, and want neither meat nor drink till we

return. Glum !'—the pilot came up hastily when
called—'you shall go to the ships and see that last
night's gale has not injured them ; let them be drawn
higher up the beach, if needs be. Report at once to
me in the wood, or to Rolf, should I have left the
tree-fellers.'

'With your permission,' said Glum, 'I will stay
about the buildings ; there is much to be done.'

'No, Glum,' answered the master, 'I require you
to examine the vessels ; no one else is so competent.
You must go.'

'May I speak a word in your ear?' asked the
pilot, glancing uneasily at Thorstein the Fox.

Gregorius rose and went with him to the further
end of the hall.

'You may be sure,' whispered Glum, ' that fellow
is a rogue; his tale is a lie. Beware of the man.
The Fox may be the most sagacious of all animals,
but it is also a great thief and rascal. Alf had but
one son.'

Gregorius smiled, and said :

'You are mistaken, friend ; you sought to persuade
me that our good neighbour, the priest, was a cut-
throat. However, to satisfy you, Leif and Arir shall
remain, and there will be others working hard by.'

'Thorstein the Fox has an injured leg, has he ?'
asked Glum. 'I doubt that ;' and, without awaiting
a reply, he left the hall.

In order to explain what we have related, it will
be necessary to narrate briefly what occurred after
Gudruna had dismissed her son on what proved to
be a bootless errand. Thorstein the Fox was one of

the dependents of the Hraunvellir family, and he was
treated with considerable familiarity, as he served,
much in the same way as Glum at Oræfa, in a
double capacity—as confidential messenger, and
sometimes adviser, or as family genealogist—and
was supposed to be well acquainted with every
detail of the pedigree, and able to relate all the
amous deeds of the family. These he was bound
to teach his son, in order that his place might be
supplied for the ensuing generation. Thorstein
was the man Gudruna instinctively summoned to
her aid the moment Eric had left Hraunvellir. She
explained succinctly to him the circumstances,
mentioned Eric's confession of love for the daughter
of his father's murderer, her determination to revenge
her husband and child, and to frustrate her son's
intentions towards the girl, which would inevitably
blunt his feelings of animosity to her kindred.
Thorstein at once fell in with Gudruna's views, and
promised to bring the young woman to Hraunvellir
as expeditiously as possible.

'Do not let me see her,' said the lady, 'for, look
you, I had kept back this dagger that I might use it
upon her; but I will not: I do not war with women.
Carry her off to my sister at Kirkjubæ, and let her
become my sister's slave.'

After having received his injunctions, Thorstein
had gone forth to find a couple of men to accompany
him, and while thus occupied Wielund had returned
to fetch his sword, and consequently was enabled to
give an idea to his young master of what was
meditated.

Having thus cleared up the difficulties which might have confused the reader, we will return to the Fox, as he lay by the fire in the hall of Oræfadal.

A considerable portion of the morning passed, and Thorstein remained dozing quietly over the embers. Ingibjorg, in the meantime, occupied herself at household work in the same apartment, without giving a thought to the sleeping man, until she saw him sit up, rub his eyes, and growl. The Fox looked cautiously round the hall, and, having satisfied himself that Ingibjorg was the only occupant beside himself, he beckoned to her. The girl dropped her work, and approached him to inquire whether he were in need of anything; but, without giving her time to ask, he muttered, looking keenly into her face :

'There is someone in the hills wishes to speak to you; I met him on my way hither, and he commissioned me to give you this;' Thorstein felt in his breast and drew out a gold cap-pin.

Ingibjorg blushed, and her heart beat very fast.

'Who can that be ?' she asked, in a low, tremulous voice.

Thorstein smiled grimly.

'I think you know him—his name is Eric.'

The girl blushed a deeper red.

'What can he desire to say to me ?' she inquired.

'That is no concern of mine,' replied the man. 'I know nothing about that; he begged me to tell you that he was among the hills, and wished particularly to see you, even if for a small moment.'

' Where is he ?' Ingibjorg asked, in a tone so low as hardly to be audible. ' Is he at the fountain ?'

' Fountain ? No, he is not at the fountain. Come with me ; I will show you where he is.'

' I cannot go,' said the girl, drawing back.

' That is your concern, not mine,' growled Thorstein, re-seating himself. ' But he told me that if you would not consent to speak with him now, for a few short moments only—and he has urgent cause for asking this—he will leave Iceland, and you will never see him again.'

' But,' said Ingibjorg, trembling, ' what can make him so anxious ? I am sure I never gave him cause to be jealous. Leave Iceland ! What can he mean? I have met him three or four times at the fountain, that is all.'

Thorstein the Fox folded his arms and leaned back on his seat.

' Will you not go and ask him what he wants and —and thank him for the hair-pin ? I shall always wear it—tell him as much,' faltered the maiden.

' No,' replied the man ill-humouredly. ' I'll do as he asked, and nothing more. I will show you where he is, but carry no messages.'

' I do not like quite——' whispered the girl. ' What would my father say ?'

' What did he say to your letting Eric escape?' asked Thorstein, looking sharply into the girl's eyes.

Ingibjorg retreated to her work, and pretended to be intent upon it. The Fox rolled himself up by the fire, and disposed himself to sleep once more. The girl raised her eyes towards him now and then, and

THERE WAS A HEAD LOOKING TOWARDS HER FROM BEHIND THAT PILE OF ROCKS.

at last ventured on some trifling remark, which was
responded to with a grunt only. Then ensued a
prolonged pause. Ingibjorg made sad mistakes in
her work; at last she flung it aside, and asked
nervously :

'You will not carry a message for me ?'

'No,' was the reply; 'I carry no messages. I
have a bad memory; I forget what is told me.
Besides, I have sprained my foot; if I had not
promised to do so, I would not consent even to
conduct you to the young man.'

'Well,' said Ingibjorg, rising, 'I will go with you ;
but Leif shall accompany us.' She called through
the door, and a man came in.

'Leif,' she said, 'I want you to accompany this
good friend and me a little way into the hills.'

Thorstein rose reluctantly from his bench, and,
after a wistful glance at Magnus' sword, followed
Ingibjorg and Leif out of the hall.

No sooner were they beyond the enclosure, or
tûn, than the Fox took the lead, hobbling somewhat
rapidly up the lava-strewn slope. Some little distance had been gone, when Leif, touching his young
mistress's arm, said in a low voice :

'There was a head looking towards us from
behind that pile of rocks, but it has disappeared
now.'

'I—I dare say there was,' answered Ingibjorg, as
her heart palpitated with expectation, mingled with
fear; 'I expect someone to be there.'

Thorstein the Fox now fell back, and walked
beside the girl. The ascent became steeper. The

mass of crag to which Leif had pointed was close at hand.

' Have I much further to go ?' asked Ingibjorg.

' Not much ; beyond that rock you will find him.'

' Then I think that I will walk forward alone. Leif, you may remain here ; I am going but twenty paces ahead.   Perhaps you, friend, will remain with Leif.'

' With your permission,' answered Thorstein, ' now that I have shown you the spot, I will sit down where I am.'

' Very well,' said the girl, and went forward.

' Whom is she going to meet ?' asked Leif.

' That is no concern of mine,' replied the red-haired man. ' Look and see.'

He turned his back, and gave a sharp whistle ; at the same moment his sword was in his uplifted hand, and before Leif had time to spring out of its sweep it fell on him and wounded him. It would have killed him had he not swerved. Without bestowing another look upon him, Thorstein, now perfectly recovered from his lameness, darted after Ingibjorg, who was already in the grip of his companions. The screams and struggles of the girl were in vain ; a bandage about the mouth silenced the first, and the latter were futile in the iron grasp of Thorstein.

' Now, friends,' exclaimed the Fox gleefully, ' where are the horses ?'

Three steeds were soon brought from behind some lava blocks, where they had been tethered. Thorstein lifted Ingibjorg on his own horse, and then mounted himself. The road was rugged and uncertain, as the cavalcade could not follow the river-bed for fear of detection, but was compelled to keep up the mountain-side.

'Alf had but one son,' muttered Thorstein to himself, laughing heartily. ' I know that as well as that fellow who said so ; and also there is not, and never was, any Bjarni Elidagrimson.'

CHAPTER XVII.

CROSSING THE RIVER.

Olver to the Rescue

LVER was the first to reach the opposite bank; he was joined almost immediately by Wielund.

'The water is like ice,' said the latter, stamping, and wringing the moisture from his clothes; then, carefully wiping his sword, 'By Tyrfing, I thought it was all over with me just now; I got into a whirl of the stream, and had much ado to strike through it.'

'Where is Eric?—he has not come on shore yet,' said Olver, looking at the water. 'He is not as strong as we are. I wish him well across.'

At that moment there came a call—almost a cry—from the river. The men looked down the stream, and indistinctly saw their young master battling with the current—vainly, as it appeared, for he was being rapidly swept down. Olver and Wielund ran along the bank, shouting in reply. An eddy took him, swung him round vehemently, and then carried him off.

'I must in,' said Olver, 'if it cost me my life.' And disencumbering himself of his sword, he tore off his clothes.

Another cry! a block of ice bore down the current, was whirled round once, and Eric disappeared beneath it.

'Stop, Olver, stop!' Wielund exclaimed, clutching his companion's shoulder, 'for the love of heaven, don't attempt it; there's no further use!'

'I must,' answered Olver; 'let go—leave hold of me, will you?' He struggled to free himself from the grasp of his friend.

'No, you shall not go,' said Wielund with a shrill, agitated voice. 'Did you see that ice-block strike him? He cannot have escaped—you will not be able to save him; Olver, you shall not!'

The two men strove desperately with each other, till Olver, bursting away, rushed down the bank again, calling loudly to his master.

'Olver, it is folly!' shouted Wielund, running at his heels.

'I see him—I see him!' screamed Olver, still running; 'I'll save him yet.'

Wielund saw Eric, or what might be Eric. In the middle of the stream lay a sandy bank covered with wild corn and a few heather sprigs. The river had risen over a good part of this patch, or had carried it away; it still, however, broke the current half-way across. Eric had caught at, and was clinging to, the moist sedge and grass; on each side, the torrent whirled past with greater velocity in its contracted beds, and further down, at only a little distance, it clashed with the salt breakers. Olver hesitated at this point, for the violence of the stream was more than he could possibly combat and overcome. He ran back, that the current might carry him to the same spot.

'If he loose his grasp, or the weed give way before I reach him, God have mercy on his soul,' he said, and stepped into the water.

'Stop, Olver,' called Wielund, flinging himself in after him, and again holding him back.

'Loose me!' said the other savagely, and struck at him.

'No,' gasped Wielund; 'only listen—hark! I hear horses' hoofs behind us; ride in after Eric.'

As he spoke, a priest, mounted on a powerful black mare, trotted rapidly up to the river-side. The two men sprang on shore; Olver half forced, half besought the rider to dismount, leaped on the animal's back, and plunged into the water. The priest ran to the brink, caught hold of Wielund, and with agitation asked what was the matter.

'Look, only look!' was the sole reply.

The horse swam lustily through the foam which had gathered on the river inlet; then with a snort it struck into the main current. It was caught at once, it seemed to bound; it turned, and was tossed along.

Wielund darted down the bank, cheering loudly. The priest saw the peril, and held his breath.

The brave creature resigned itself to the sweep of the torrent. Olver sat firmly on its back, upright, and the reins firmly grasped. The sand ridge was neared; Eric still clung to the tangled sedge. In the fork of the stream, where it divided above the sand-bank, the water seemed sufficiently tranquil; could Olver but reach that, he might land on the ridge and draw his master on shore; he turned the mare's head in that direction; the animal struggled violently; it saw safety as clearly as did its rider; its nostrils dilated, every muscle in its well-knit body wrought; it was at the point, the waves danced; every vein in Olver's body stood forth like whipcord; his eye was fixed on the grassy strip, his teeth were clenched, his lips compressed and white, his hand firm, unwavering on the rein, his knees clasping the flanks tightly, as if his thews had contracted into iron. Foam bubbles leaped and wheeled off on each side; a bramble was floating before him, coiled up; it was tossed up and down, sucked in; again emerging unwoven, it trailed out; like an arrow it shot away. Wielund stood silent; the critical moment was come. The priest fell on his knees, and great drops of sweat beaded his brow.

The horse and rider seemed for one moment motionless; first slowly, then faster, ever faster still they glided on; one wild shriek from the horse—such as those animals are only known to utter when in

despair—and they were dashed away. Olver had
not lost presence of mind for an instant; as he was
carried past, he caught Eric's outstretched arm.
Wielund and the priest saw that, and then they ran
down the river-side; rocks and rubble checked their
speed, they lost sight of those in the river; a thick,
blinding rain fell; the opposite bank was invisible.
The shore became more sandy near the sea.

Suddenly Wielund gave a shout of joy; he saw
Olver kneeling on the shingle beside Eric, who lay
prostrate upon it; and hard by, trembling from its
efforts, was the black mare.

Olver had caught Eric by the arm; the current had
swept horse and rider and Eric down and cast them
on the sandy bank or bar where the river met the
sea.

'Deo gratias!' exclaimed the priest.

'He is not dead,' said Olver, as Wielund stooped
over Eric; 'but you see he has a bad gash on his
head, where the ice struck him.'

'Let us carry him to the cottage we noticed on
our way yesterday; it is close at hand,' said Wielund,
lifting Eric's head.

Olver raised the feet, and the two men bore their
young master, while the priest followed, leading the
mare. In a short space of time a fisherman's hovel
was reached; the owner lighted a fire, and Eric was
laid on a bench beside it. While Olver bandaged
the wound in the head, the house-wife warmed the
soles of the young man's feet, and the priest conversed with the fisherman.

'Is there no means of crossing the river?' asked

the priest. 'I must pass to the further side, as I am on an errand of importance.'

'The water is too high to allow of safe passage,' answered the man.

'And you had better not venture the horse into the river again to-day, even at the ford,' advised Wielund.

'I must hasten to the good Father Swerker as soon as possible,' said the priest.

'I know him well,' observed the fisherman; 'he and I were playmates as children. I have been friendly with him ever since, and now we are both getting on to be old men. I do not believe there is a holier man in all Iceland; his mother taught him while quite young those blessed truths which are now his very life; the mother's heart is her child's school-room! You should know the father as I do, to see how kind and good he is. To be sure, he may have his weaknesses, but they are sinless ones, and that is more than the best of us can say.'

'Then, as you are his friend,' said the priest, 'you will be glad to hear my errand. I am on my way to Father Swerker to announce to him his appointment as abbot of the Kirkjubæ monastery.'

The fisherman's face brightened with a glow of joy and pride.

'Others know his value, then, as well as myself,' he said.

'When and how can I cross the river?' asked the priest again.

'The water will fall rapidly, unless we have more rain; and you may safely wade through to-morrow,

or perhaps this evening; then I will accompany
you.'

There was no help for this delay, and the
messenger was obliged to remain contented where
he was.

Eric slowly recovered from insensibility, and towards mid-day revived sufficiently to be able to walk,
but he had not strength to undertake the return
journey to Hraunvellir. He was restless and excited,
and despatched Wielund to watch for Thorstein. He
was too late, however; the Fox with Ingibjorg had
passed that way just before the hour of noon.

CHAPTER XVIII.

CROSSING ANOTHER RIVER.

Glum discovers

GLUM returned slowly from the boats; he was absorbed in his own thoughts, and did not raise his eyes from the ground, while every now and then he shook his head and muttered between his teeth. He kept some way up the hillside, so as to avoid the overflowed water-meadows; the wood in which Gregorius was engaged lay higher up the valley, and the pilot had no intention of going to

his master until he had visited the farm to have
another talk with Thorstein, and, if possible, to
come to blows with him.

'Alf had but one son,' muttered the pilot, kicking
at the stones as he walked. 'I should like to prove
it with my sword-point on that rascal.'

Suddenly he stopped, and started back from a
trail of fresh blood on the sand and coarse grass.
His eyes in another moment caught sight of Leif,
prostrate a few paces below him. Glum sprang to
his side, and saw the fearful gash inflicted by
Thorstein's weapon. The face of the wounded man
was gray, and drawn with pain; he had crawled
down the hillside as far as his strength would allow
him, and lay, faint from loss of blood, where the
pilot found him. Without a moment's hesitation,
Glum dashed over rock and stone to the river's edge,
filled his sealskin cap with water, and returned to
Leif, whose breast, convulsed and throbbing,
struggled for breath. The cool water somewhat
revived him, and his eyes fixed themselves on Glum,
but the words he strove to articulate died in his
throat. The pilot lifted his fellow-servant's head
upon his knee, and continued moistening his forehead, or wiping the blood from the edges of the
wide unstanchable wound.

'Comrade,' said Glum, 'do you feel a little better
now?'

Leif's eyelids quivered, his lips moved, and he
lifted his already numbed and bloodless fingers to
make some sign.

'I cannot understand you, friend,' said Glum;

'but if you want to know what I think of your condition, I will tell you frankly—you have not an hour to live.'

Leif raised his livid fingers towards his lips—the fingers of his left hand, for the right shoulder, with all its tendons, was cut through, so that the arm hung paralyzed, the hand trailing on the black sand.

'Water?' asked the pilot, and he poured some of the ice-cold draught down the dying man's throat. He seemed to revive directly.

'Glum,' he whispered.

'Well,' replied the pilot, 'tell me whether I have to revenge you on that rascal Thorstein the Fox. Oh, I suspected the fellow from the moment that he said Alf had two sons. Was he your murderer?'

Leif gave a feeble assent to the inquiry.

'He has carried off Ingibjorg,' he murmured. 'Never mind me; go after him at once.'

'There is time enough,' observed Glum with an unusually cheerful voice. 'Gregorius will find out *now* that I am no false prophet. Is there anything I can do for you after you are dead, friend?'

'Nothing,' muttered Leif; his lungs beat and quivered as a spasm contracted his breast.

'You have no particular fancy for any place to be buried in?' asked Glum.

The dying man slightly shook his head.

'Fetch me a priest, for God's sake,' he said in a clearer voice than before—almost with a cry.

Glum looked distressed as he replied: 'That, comrade, I cannot do; there is none whom I could bring in time to see you alive.'

'I cannot die,' gasped Leif; 'I must not, will not.'

'There is no priest nearer than the river-mouth,' said Glum. 'Is there anything on your mind or conscience?'

'Then fetch me the master. I must speak with him,' said the dying man in a low, tremulous whisper.

The pilot remained silent, and looked uncertainly into the face of his fellow, wiped with his finger a smear of blood from his cheek, drew the clogged hair off the forehead. A film spread over the up-turned eyes.

'Halloo!' was shouted from the area behind the farm. 'Glum, is that you?'

Glum looked up, and saw Thorarin leap the moat and run up the hill. He beckoned to him to hasten.

'Is that the master?' asked Leif, reviving, and an anxious tremor ran through his limbs—not through all—not the right arm that was already dead.

The pilot shook his head.

'Glum,' murmured the dying man, 'there is something I would have said to the master that I should have told before. Glum! I didn't think to die now; I have put off and off——' His voice became feebler. Glum thought he said, 'Pray for me,' but he was not sure.

'What is the matter?' asked Thorarin, coming up panting. 'Why, Glum, how has this happened? Leif, is that you? By Thor, what a gash!'

The pilot beckoned silence with his finger, and then pointed to Leif's face. The cheeks were ashy pale, the bloodless lips twitched nervously, and the eyelids quivered; the short, broken breath hissed through the clenched teeth; the left hand picked and clawed at the sand, but the feet remained motionless: they were dead now. Thorarin stood startled, yet quite quiet, by the side. Glum pressed the head tighter in his hands, and the breast rose and fell, fast and short.

'Leif,' said he into the ear, 'have you no last word to say?'

'Who is that has come?' asked the man, suddenly reviving; then he added faintly: 'You'll revenge me, Glum?'

'With most hearty good-will,' answered the pilot. 'Do you desire anything further?'

'I'll haunt you if you fail. I shall be a wandering, an unblessed spirit,' he said.

'God forbid!' exclaimed Glum, horror-struck.

'Is he come yet?' asked again the poor man. 'There is something I desired to say. It is——'

Then there was a last throe, a tearing at, and gathering of, the dust with the one hand, a vehement struggle to turn on one side, a whistling breath in short gasps; Glum's arms were drawn tighter round him in that last agony; then a low sigh—a low, awful sigh, a bitter sigh—and the muscles relaxed, the weight dragged heavily on Glum's arms, and the head sank back on his bosom; the sand ran out of the left clenched hand in a little heap, dust to dust. The wind moaned among the tufts of parched grass, and the river rushed by down in the vale, and its discoloured waters lost themselves in the ocean.

'It is all over now,' said Glum. Then he sprang

to his feet and grasped Thorarin's arm. 'There is
not a moment to be lost now; your sister is carried
off. We must to horse and pursue.'

'To death, if maybe,' said Thorarin. 'Come
Glum, let us to Hraunvellir at once.'

'Hraunvellir!' exclaimed Glum. 'Why there?'

'Never mind; I will explain on the way; you
bring the horses in and bridle them. I will fetch
the arms and send off a message to my father.'

'Stop,' said Glum. 'You are sure she is carried
to Hraunvellir?'

'Quite,' answered the youth.

'Then, in Heaven's name,' exclaimed the pilot,
'let us go on foot across the glacier; it will be
quicker than riding round by Hòf.'

By this time the house was reached. Thorarin
entered the hall, grasped a shield, and Magnus'
sword—the sword which our readers will remember; and, after having armed Glum and sent
off a message to Gregorius in the wood, both sallied
forth.

CHAPTER XIX.

THE TIGRESS'S DEN.

GUDRUNA sat next morning in the hall alone, engaged in her household work, the sun shining in at the open door, and many flies gaily sporting in the yellow beam. A shadow in the doorway made her look up: Thorarin and Glum walked in and approached her.

'Woman,' said the former, 'we have come for our sister. Where is she?'

'And who may your sister be?' asked Gudruna, rising proudly from her seat.

'Answer me!' shouted Thorarin, clashing his sword against the floor, 'where is she?'

Gudruna's lip curled, her eye fell on the sword which the youth had lowered, and her veins darkened and swelled.

'Well?' called Thorarin impetuously, 'will you not let me know whether she be here or not?'

'I know not whom you mean,' answered Gudruna; 'go round the house and look for yourself.'

'We shall do that without your leave,' said Glum. 'Let us search at once, Thorarin.'

'It is well,' answered the young man, leaving the hall.

The two hunted through every nook of the farm, but found no traces of Ingibjorg.

'We have made a mistake,' said Glum. 'Hark at that woman blowing a horn! We should have bound her, fools that we were! She will call all the farm-men about us.'

'There can be no mistake in our coming here,' said Thorarin. 'Father Swerker warned Magnus and me that these people were meditating mischief; and, though we see not my sister here, hereabouts she must be.'

'The foul fiends take that horn!' exclaimed the pilot. 'Come on, we must not stay; we shall never escape if we do not go at once.'

'That is right!' cried Thorarin joyfully, as he looked out of the window. 'I see several men coming; we shall not get away without sport.'

'More sport than we wish for!' growled Glum.

'Come! let us at them!' gleefully shouted the youth, bounding from the door among the farm-men.

A yell of exultation greeted him from Gudruna, who stood on a large lava-block which lay in the corner of the enclosure before the house. 'Cut those two down, friends ! Spare them not, the murderers !' she screamed, in one hand brandishing the dagger which she had taken from her son, in the other the horn ; then she blew a long, triumphant blast, and shouted again to her men. Her black hair burst from beneath her cap and flew about wildly in the wind, and still she called and blew blasts on her horn. Thorarin and the Pilot could get no further than the door. A knot of men, armed with various hastily-caught-up weapons, surrounded and hemmed them in.

'Stop !' called Glum, with a voice like a trumpet. All remained still. 'We have come herè under a mistake. The bonder of Oræfa-dal has lost his daughter, and we have come in search of her, thinking she might be here. Let us go in peace, and do not let blood be shed for naught.'

'Cut them down !' cried Gudruna, and then she blew a shrill flourish on the cow-horn. Thorarin's sword was the first to fall as he rushed among the assailants, whirling it in arcs of light above his head. Glum, with greater caution, planted himself against the wall and fought only on the defensive. Clubs and stakes were of no avail before the sweeps of Fireheart as it flashed and fell, and the joy of fighting began to flame and swell in Thorarin's breast. What his brave heart had long panted for was now come to pass, and, in a hand-to-hand fight with superior numbers, the happiness of a wild

nature, unsubdued, like a rising fountain, bore him
up and on in a transport of true joy. Fireheart
sent no longer silver gleams in the sun, but flashed
lurid and purple as the blood ran down the blade
and over the hilt. Down went clubs, a spear fell
severed by a single blow; some men dropped on the
already sprinkled ground, others staggered as drunken
men to the rear, and sank at the foot of the rock on
which Gudruna stood.

'Strike that woman-fiend down!' shouted Glum to
his young master.

'Heaven forbid!' exclaimed Thorarin; 'I have
work here more suited to a man. Let women fight
with women.' He backed towards the wall, for he
had already received some wounds from behind as
he impetuously dashed forwards regardless of the
rear, and every now and then a laugh burst from him
as his assailants shrank before each sweep of his
sword.

A great stone whirled through the air and crashed
against the wall above him; Gudruna had hurled
it from her elevated position. Before she could
throw another, Thorarin had folded his mantle
about his left arm and had raised it to protect
his head. Another stone was cast and hit him on
the arm. Fireheart was a two-handed sword, and
could ill be managed by one hand alone, so that the
farm-servants began to gain ground as his one arm
was momentarily disabled.

'Get into the doorway!' called Glum, and with
frantic sweeps of his blade he carved his way
forwards towards the lava-block on which Gudruna

GLUM, SUPPORTED ON HIS LEFT HAND, WHEELING HIS GORY SWORD ROUND HIM.

was mounted. Thorarin followed the pilot's advice, and was somewhat relieved from the press of numbers, partly by his position, partly by Glum having drawn off several of the farm-servants, who flew to defend their mistress. Glum's advance was not rapid, for the men thronged about him, and in another moment Thorarin heard him shout for help. The young man quitted the door at once, swept from his path those who opposed him, and came upon Glum, who had fallen, but was supported on his left hand, wheeling his gory sword round him, so that none could reach him—now flashing before, then with a back stroke making the men in his rear leap out of the way. Thorarin planted himself with his back to Glum, so as to be his defence in the rear, trusting to the sturdy pilot to keep off those in front; and thus the struggle continued unremittingly. Gudruna flung another mass of splintered lava, but with such uncertain aim that it felled one of her own servants. At that moment a scream from Gudruna arrested the hands of the combatants.

' Eric ! my son, my son !' exclaimed the maddened mother; ' you are come in time to strike the last blow and to rescue old Fireheart !'

The farm-servants, dispirited at their want of success, and cowed by the superior courage of Thorarin and the pilot, as well as glad of a moment's pause, fell back on every side.

Eric, Olver, and Wielund stood in the entrance to the enclosure, amazed at the scene of turmoil and blood before their eyes.

' Eric, dear son !' Gudruna cried, leaping from the

rock, ' Eric! our foes are here, Fireheart is here ;
there is much blood to be revenged now. Go on, dear
son, and with one stroke wipe out our vengeance.'

' Mother !' said Eric, in a low, thrilling voice,
' where is the maiden—where is Ingibjorg ?'

' Never mind now, son ; beat those haughty ones
down.'

' Where is Ingibjorg ?' asked Eric again, planting
himself before his mother.

' Look, look ! see all this blood, these wounded
men !   By Loki, these two men have defied and
set us all at naught.   Eric, I bid thee finish this
strife.'

' Where is Ingibjorg ?' asked Eric again, firmly,
and with knit brows.   ' I shall not lift hand against
them till I know.'

' Dead, Eric, dead !' yelled Gudruna, springing on
the lava-block again.

Eric took his sword, doubled, and snapped it
across his knee, then threw the fragments at his
mother's feet.   Bursting with ungovernable rage, the
wretched woman lifted the horn to her lips, but her
breath was not powerful enough to sound it.

' Go !' said Eric to Thorarin and Glum ; ' I have
no further any quarrel with you.'

' They shall not go !' vociferated Gudruna ; ' help,
you men—help to stay them.'

The men stood in perplexity, doubting to whom
they owed prior allegiance—to the mother or to the
son.

' Go at once,' said Eric calmly, to Thorarin and
Glum.   ' I will protect you.'

' They shall not go ; I can prevent that !' shrieked
Gudruna, bounding from the rock, brushing through
the line of farm-servants, and springing on Thorarin
with her uplifted dagger.

The young man warded off the blow with his
sword, and with his left hand flung the woman
reeling and staggering from him. Olver caught
and restrained her in his firm grasp, till Thorarin
had raised Glum from the ground, bound a strip from
his cloak round his knee, which a sword had gashed,
and had left the court supporting his wounded
companion.

Then Olver allowed his mistress to break away
from him, and rushing into the hall, she flung herself, weeping with disappointed rage, on the high
bench by the fire. With a stern face Eric followed
and approached her. His mother remained tossing
her head buried in her arms and sobbing con-
vulsively; she would not notice him, and he stood
cold and hardened at her side without speaking.
Olver came in and said, ' Master, what is to be done
with the dead ?'

' Bury them at once.' The man left the hall.

' Well, son ?' said Gudruna, looking up.

' Woman,' answered Eric, 'think no more of me
as a son ; I cast the thought of mother from me.'

' And I that of son !' exclaimed Gudruna, dashing
her feet on the ground, ' when that son is a coward,
and will not avenge his father.'

' That is wiped off in *her* blood,' answered Eric,
with faltering voice.

' What ?' cried Gudruna scornfully, ' the murder

of brave Onund blotted out by the blood of a paltry girl!'

Eric's hands clenched, and his eyes sparkled. 'By that blow you have destroyed all my heart's joys, and made me for ever your enemy.'

Gudruna remained silent and bit her fingers till they bled. Her face was horrible: the black eyebrows united in one lowering band, the purple veins of her brow all but bursting, the cheeks livid, and the lips quivering with impotent rage.

'Woman,' said Eric resolutely, 'I shall send for Thorstein the Fox. I know that he has been your instrument; and if he will not tell all I want to know, aye, and if what you said be true, I will hew him to pieces before your eyes.'

Then, walking to the door, he called Olver. The man came up instantly.

'Bring Thorstein the Fox into the hall at once,' ordered Eric.

'He is not here,' answered Olver. 'The others have been telling me that he has not returned.'

'Not returned!' exclaimed Eric, turning to his mother. 'How is that?'

Gudruna looked up suddenly, and said, 'I will tell you all, Eric; only promise me to pursue those two men and bring me their heads.'

'I will promise nothing,' replied the sub-deacon. 'Nothing, till I know that Ingibjorg is alive.'

'If I tell you that she is so, and if I promise to give her up to you, will you swear——'

'I will swear anything!' interrupted Eric, the colour rising again to his hitherto ashy cheeks.

' You will follow after those two who have but just escaped ; you will hew them down that they may never rise again ; you will bring me back Fireheart, that dear sword ; and, when I require you, you will come with me to Oræfa-dal and burn the house down !'

' Anything, everything, mother !' gasped Eric, clasping her hands in his own, and pressing them till the wounded fingers bled again.

' Then go after those two at once ; the girl lives, and is at my sister's, the lady Steinvor of Laug, near Kirkjubæ. Quick, Eric, quick ! or they will escape you.'

The youth uttered a shout of joy and left the hall. Olver and Wielund answered his call at once, and followed him as he led them, with hasty steps, from the court in the direction taken by Thorarin and the pilot.

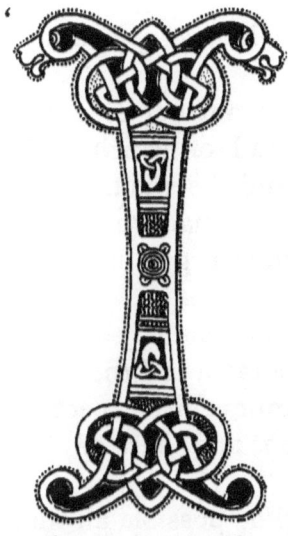

'CANNOT go much further, Thorarin,' said Glum. 'I must rest as soon as we reach the summit of the hill.'

'You must push on, friend,' said the young man, 'for I see that lad who lately saved us and two others coming after us as fast as they can, and that bodes little good.'

'Can you carry me?' asked the pilot. 'If we can reach that hill of lava we can hold our ground for some time against them. I am fresh and ready enough for another hand-to-hand bout; my leg alone prevents me from moving actively.'

Thorarin lifted the pilot on his back, and ran up the slope till he reached the mass of lava Glum had referred to; there he dropped his burden, and leaned back against the crag, somewhat out of breath.

'We are quite safe,' exclaimed Glum complacently. 'Look yonder!'

Ascending from the vale on the further side was a party of horsemen, at the head of which rode Gregorius. Thorarin shouted, and the moment his father caught sight of him, made signals to him to increase his speed. The old bonder urged his horse forward, and was soon at his son's side.

As soon as Eric and his companions saw the strong reinforcement come to Thorarin and the pilot, they turned back hastily to Hraunvellir, expecting that the party would gallop on and besiege the house.

Thorarin related as succinctly as possible all that had taken place.

His father nodded and said: 'I have gathered sufficient information on my way to know for certain that Ingibjorg is not at Hraunvellir, but has been carried across this broad sheet of water in a boat, in the direction of Kirkjubæ. We must send there at once; I came on in the expectation of finding you in trouble or in danger. I wish you now to traverse the Lomagnupr, and make the best of your way to Kirkjubæ. I hear that Father Swerker has been appointed abbot there, and has crossed the water this morning; he will be able to assist you in your search. Take three men as companions and assistants, my son, and God be with you.'

'Will you ride on to Hraunvellir, father?' asked Thorarin.

' To what end ?   We have established nothing as yet, except that Ingibjorg is not there.'

' But I know that the woman-fiend at yonder farm has been the means of my sister's abduction.'

' When we are convinced of that, I shall summon her and her son before a Thing; but now, the first matter to be considered is the recovery of Ingibjorg,' replied Gregorius.

' Farewell, then, father.   I must leave Glum with you; his wound will prevent him from accompanying me.   Alf and Einar, follow me at once; there is no time to be lost.'

Thorarin hurried to the water's side with his two comrades, and skirted the shore until he found a fisherman's cottage, where he obtained a boat, and the men crossed the Lomagnupr estuary with rapid sweeps of their oars.

Gregorius watched them from the heights till the boat shot behind a low sandy island, and could be no longer seen.   Then he turned his horse's head, and, followed by the rest of his servants and Glum, rode back in the direction of Hòf.

Thorarin stranded the little bark at the nearest point of land, and, leaving the shore, made inquiries on all sides after his sister and Thorstein the Fox. He soon gathered sufficient information to justify his advancing towards Kirkjubæ; but, as the day closed in, and he was wearied out with his exertions, he was compelled to spend the night at a little farm, at no great distance from the fiord he had just crossed.

We will return to Eric, who, on seeing the party

of Gregorius ascend the hill, deemed it expedient to return in haste to Hraunvellir, and prepare for defence, in the event of an assault, which he had cause to expect. But as time passed, and the bonder did not appear with his men at the farm gates, and when a scout reported that he had seen Gregorius and his attendants ride back in the direction of Oræfa-dal, Eric dismissed his servants, their arms were replaced in the hall, and he seated himself at his mother's side.

'Well, son,' said the lady, 'it was not your fault that those two escaped you at last, and I forgive you. Join with me now, and to-morrow night, or the next to that at latest, let us surround Oræfa-dal, and burn the farm to the ground.'

'Not yet, mother,' answered Eric. 'Before I do anything else, I must ride after Ingibjorg and bring her here.'

'It is folly,' cried Gudruna, stamping impatiently on the ground. 'She is the daughter of your father's murderer; remember that, and hate her.'

'I cannot,' answered Eric. 'Ingibjorg shall be my wife—she, and no other woman in Iceland. I vow to you, mother, that if harm happens to her, and you hinder me, I will leave for Greenland, and you will never see me more. I know you, and how soon you would be free of her or anyone you hated; but I promise you that if I lose Ingibjorg, you shall lose me. Mother, my heart is bound up in her. I leave you in order to seek her, and, when next you see me, she shall be with me. Farewell.'

' Then I shall burn down Oræfa-dal without you,'
growled Gudruna.

Eric left the hall, summoned Wielund to accompany him on horseback, and rode along the shore to
the boatman's cottage, intending to cross the frith
that same evening. There, however, he learned that
the skiff had been already rowed across by some
strangers, and was not likely to return till the following morning. The sub-deacon was much irritated at
this hindrance, and he spent the rest of the evening
in fruitless searches for another boat. It was not
till nightfall that he procured one, near Hòf; and
then the darkness precluded all attempts at crossing.
He was constrained to postpone his further journey
till daybreak.

It thus happened that on the following day
Thorarin started from where he had spent the night,
about the same time that Eric began to cross the
fiord, both bound for the same destination, but
Thorarin in advance of his adversary by several
hours.

Eric's suspicions had been aroused by what he
had heard at the boatman's hovel, and he inquired
on the opposite side of the water as to who had
crossed on the previous day, and as to the direction
they had taken. He was soon convinced that his
enemy was at no very great distance ahead, and he
redoubled his speed, so as to overtake him.

CHAPTER XXI

THE INSTALLATION.

IRKJUBÆ was in commotion. People from all the neighbourhood had been streaming in from an early hour, and the emerald meadows around the monastery were covered with peasantry and persons of rank. The men were in their war accoutrements. They conversed in groups, their shields lying against the church walls, the orbs gaily coloured red or white, or spangled with gold stars on a blue ground. The descendant of Kjartan, so famous in Saga, was present with his ancestor's buckler, from the field of which blazed a gilt cross, and beside it lay the shield that had anciently belonged to Olaf of the Salmon-River. It was decorated with a gold lion on a scarlet ground. The women, in gaudy dresses,

covered with a profusion of gold ornaments and
chains, from which were suspended medals and
amulets, sat and span from their distaffs on the
scattered blocks of obsidian, or crowded round
Eric of Waterdale, who had married the grand-
daughter of the great Icelandic historian Snorro
Sturlason. This man was famous for his knowledge
of the history of his country, and his acquaintance
with the heroic legends of the pre-Christian period—
legends which were gradually dying out.

'He is going to relate the story of Vœlund the
Forger,' ran through the assembly, and mothers
called for their children that they might come and
listen to the tale. Some of the men approached,
and leaned on their broad two-handed swords.

'You must pay attention, Ingibjorg,' said a
matron in a dusky cassock, unconfined at the waist
and richly embroidered on the breast, her head-dress
much resembling a monstrous corkscrew. 'You
must attend, for my sister Gudruna, of Hraunvellir,
and I claim descent from this same Vœlund—a
very great and very wicked man he was—hardly a
man altogether; something of the elf was in his
blood. My brother-in-law had a sword, fabricated
by Vœlund, and called Fireheart; it was given him
by the King of Scotland. It was a good and thirsty
blade, but I know not where it is now. He took it
to Norway with him, and never returned. It was a
great loss.'

Ingibjorg, who was at her side, turned her head
petulantly away.

'I want to know nothing about it,' she said. 'You

have no right to keep me here. Let me go back to Oræfa-dal.'

'No, no,' answered Gudruna's sister; 'you have been entrusted to my care, and for excellent reasons I doubt not, though I do not know them. I intend keeping you by me till Thorstein the Fox brings me a message what further is to be done with you. Now hold your tongue; it is of no use fretting: you cannot escape. If you attempted to do so, I would have you bound. Now hearken, the Saga-man is about to begin.'

Eric of Waterdale rang out a harsh chord on his Langspiel, a curious musical instrument like a narrow box, bulging on one side near the end, at which was a sound-vent; over it were stretched three strings. In the open air the music was somewhat pleasing.

'Hearken, hearken, neighbours,' the scald exclaimed, 'hearken to the relation of the deeds of Vœlund, the mighty forger who wrought the sword Durandal for Charlemagne, and Mimung for King Thidric of Berne.'

There was silence among the audience, the only commotion being caused by a restive babe in its mother's arms. By general acclamation the woman was ordered to withdraw with her nursling, and the scald began :

'This is the song of Vœlund the Forger, who dwelt in Ulf-dal by the Bear Tarn :

'"Vœlund the Forger dug deep for gold,
And fashioned seven hundred rings ;
Then strung them all on the osier bough
Where the reed bird resting sings ;

12

And they tinkled as bells, when raved the gale,
And they glinted as stars in the moon-gleam pale.

'" Vœlund the Forger went out to chase,
    When the morn broke wan and gray ;
King Niduth came with his forty men,
    And he stole one ring away ;
Then the warriors crouched in the bushes around,
And their beards streamed over the frozen ground.

'" Vœlund the Forger came back at eve
    And kindled a roaring fire ;
He roasted a bear at the flaring logs,
    The flames gushed higher and higher ;
Then stringing his rings on a bearskin thong,
He marvelled to find that one was gone.

'" Vœlund the Forger lay down to sleep,
    His soul fluttered far away ;
Up rose from the bushes the forty knights
    And they bound him as he lay ;
He strove till the cordage cut to the bone,
But Niduth joyously bore him home.

'" Niduth the king has hewn off his feet ;
    Though the Forger no more can stand,
Yet merrily roars the forge's fire,
    And he wields his stalwart hand.
On a stilly night one could hear the crank
Of the bellows, and list his anvil's clank.

'" Vœlund the Forger toiled amain,
    When the storm went sobbing by.
The clouds overhead were tinged with red,
    The forge-fire flared to the sky.
The hammer flew and the bellows blew,
And the echoes clattered all the night through."

You must understand that Niduth was a mighty
kind of Svithiod (Sweden), that he had two sons,
princes, and a beautiful daughter, Braudvilda. And
Niduth made Vœlund fashion for him harness and
arms of war, also choice drinking horns. There was
not anywhere to be found a more perfect workman

than Vœlund; but he was lame, for the king had maimed him lest he should escape, and the song tells further—

> '" Niduth bade his daughter and sons,
>   'Oh, never, my children, go
> Where stands a forge on a tufted moor,
>   Where you hear the bellows blow ;
> Weird tools frameth an elf-king there,
> Footless, and having wild black hair." '

But the princes, moved with curiosity, traversed the dun moor, and looked in at the blacksmith's sooty window, and as says the lay—

> '" Vœlund the Forger raised his head :
>   'Forger, we come to behold
> Thy shining blades of sea-blue steel,
>   Thy chains of silver and gold ;
> Make us, we pray thee, a noble ring,
> We are the sons of Niduth the king.'
>
> '" Vœlund the Forger right grimly smiled
>   As he closed and hasped the door ;
> Then, with a blow of his sooty tongs,
>   He smote both dead on the floor.
> The raven croaked on the grimy roof,
> The falcon wheeled and screamed aloof.
>
> '" Vœlund the Forger toiled fast and hard,
>   Poured moon-white silver out ;
> He graved two chalices set with rings
>   And richly tooled them about.
> The skulls were chased in those drinking cups ;
> The king from the Forger's presents sups.
>
> '" ' Pretty Braudvilda, I give thee this cup
>   To adorn thy damsel bower.'
> The maid hath broken the silver bowl
>   While mounting her lonely tower.
> 'Ah ! woe is me ! what, alas ! have I done ?
> Swift to Vœlund, who'll mend it, I'll run.' "

Now, Vœlund had been seated on the bench outside, armed with his bow, and with his arrows he brought to the ground many a swarthy raven ; their wings he cunningly wrought into two mighty pennons, as saith the song—

> ' " Vœlund the Forger has drawn his bow,
>   And the ravens have failed in flight.
>   Mighty the pennons he frames therefrom :
>   To his sides he fits them tight.
>   Vœlund has smiled a smile ghastly and grim
>   As the princess offers the cup to him.
>
> ' " Vœlund the Forger spread out his arms.
>   ' Come, pretty maiden, to me :
>   Give me the cup from thy lily-white hand :
>   Firmly I'll weld it for thee.'
>   Away on his wings did the blacksmith soar ;
>   Niduth beheld Braudvilda no more !" '*

Before the scald had finished, the bell of the monastery church had begun to clamour in the sort of wooden framework set up in the churchyard, apart from the church, and a deacon had summoned the congregation from the top of the outer church wall, on which he stood with a wooden gong and clapper in his hands. Clerical attire was at this period somewhat more regarded than it had been in a previous century, when the Archbishop of Drontheim had to remonstrate with the priest Laurence

* Vœlund the smith has been famous throughout Europe from a remote period. He is mentioned in the elder Edda of Sæmund, in the Wilkina Saga ; also in the Anglo-Saxon poem of Beowulf, in King Alfred's translation of Boethius ; in Spencer's ' Fairy Queen,' and in common tradition as Wayland the Smith (in ' Kenilworth ') at the White Horse Vale, in Berkshire. In German romance he is mentioned in the ancient Heldenbuch, etc. ; and in many old French, Italian, and Spanish poems Vœlund answers, in many respects, to Vulcan and to Dædalus. The tradition of his cunning, his skill, his lameness, his treachery, seems common to all the Aryan race, for traces of it are found in the Vedas ; in Ceylon smiths are called by the natives Velendes.

for coming out in pink as his ordinary costume, and had, instead, to give him a sober brown coat.* The clergy now wore cassocks of coarse wool, but there was not much uniformity in their colour, although none attained to the vivid hue of that worn by Laurence. The deacon leaped from the wall, and hurried into the monastic buildings to assist in the formation of the procession.

It will perhaps be interesting to the reader to understand the construction of the church into which we are about to introduce him. Kirkjubæ was certainly one of the most important ecclesiastical centres in Iceland, and its abbot held a position of great dignity, and exercised a wide influence in the island. As might be expected, the collegiate church was considered next only to the two cathedrals in architectural merit and wealth in the ornaments connected with Divine worship. Imagine an edifice of wood, with very high-pitched roof covered with turf, where grass and buttercups grew; the side walls also banked up with turf; only the gable ends exposed, of wood painted red with ochre. The church was surrounded by a wall some eight or ten feet from it, rising to within a few feet of the main walls; this was covered in winter with a temporary roof of boards, so as to form a narrow way all round the building, and was serviceable to keep the snow and frost from the real church walls. There was a window at the west end over the door, which was covered, as soon as the frost set in, by seal-skins, and was, in fact, nothing more than a square open-

* Laurent Bishop Saga.

ing to admit light. A round window covered with parchment stood high up in the eastern gable, which was surmounted by a wooden cross daubed scarlet; the outer window splay was painted with blue and yellow zigzags. The main beams crossed, and were grotesquely carved to represent the heads of dragons. The church internally consisted of a barn-like nave without side aisles, and a choir separated from the body of the sacred edifice by an open screen of three arches of sea-drifted pine, surmounted by a gigantic cross, the whole painted red, blue, and white. On the roodloft burned numerous oil lamps, and the choir was filled with large pendent burners, which had completely blackened the roof. The altar was hewn out of a block of lava, which had stood within the foundations before the completion of the church; it had no frontals, but had the front gilded and inlaid with rock crystal. The candles in the church were composed of tallow, and the lamps filled with whale blubber, and had to be snuffed and trimmed during the service. As may be imagined, they emitted anything but a pleasant smell. But to this Icelanders were accustomed, and they hardly noticed it. Over the altar was a handsome carved wooden reredos, representing the crucifixion, richly gilded, the borders of the garments of the sacred figures beaded with garnets.

The flora of the Arctic circle is destitute of the brilliantly hued flowers which adorn our gardens, but faithful and loving hearts had 'done what they could' with the yellow poppy and common eyebright, together with tall tansies, to brighten up the

altar, and the screen and choir seats were adorned
with tiny blue gentian and meadow-sweet.

The new abbot, as a member of the Skalholt
College, was preceded by two sub-deacons from that
cathedral, vested in capes which had been lent to do
special honour to Father Swerker, and which were
considered as treasures of the cathedral-church, for
on them hangs a tale which, at the risk of tedious-
ness, I must be allowed to insert in the words of the
historian Snorro Sturlason: 'King Harald was a
generous man. It is told that in his time Magnus
Einarsson came from Iceland to be consecrated a
bishop, and the 'king received him well, and showed
him much respect. When the bishop was ready to
sail for Iceland again, and the ships were rigged out
for sea, he went to the hall where the king was
drinking, saluted him politely and warmly, and the
king received him joyfully. The queen was sitting
by the king. Then said the king, "Are you ready,
bishop, for your voyage?" He replied that he was.
The king said, "You come to us just now at a bad
time; for the tables are just removed, and there is
nothing at hand suitable to present you with. What
is there to give the bishop?" The treasurer replies,
"Sire, as far as I know, all articles of any value are
given away." Quoth the king: "Here is a drinking
goblet remaining; take this, bishop—it is not without value." The bishop expressed his thanks for
the honour shown him. Then said the queen,
"Farewell, bishop, and a happy voyage." The
king said to her, "Who ever heard of a noble lady
talking so to a bishop without giving him some-

thing?" She replies, "Sire, what have I to give him?" The king quoth, "Thou art sitting on a cushion." Thereupon this, which was covered with costly cloth, and was a valuable article, was given to the bishop. When the bishop was going away, the king took the cushion from under himself and gave it him, saying, "They have long been together." When the bishop arrived in Iceland in his see, choristers' cloaks were made of the costly cloth with which the cushions given him by the king and queen were covered; they are now in Skalholt.'*

No sooner had Ingibjorg caught sight of Father Swerker than the colour flashed into her cheeks, and through the whole service she continued in great agitation. She had heard from her keeper, the lady with the corkscrew cap, that the new abbot was named Swerker, but it had hardly occurred to the girl that he might be the friendly old priest who had spent a night at Oræfa-dal, till she saw him enter in the procession. Gudruna's sister noticed her excitement, and attributing it to want of manners, rebuked her sharply, though in an undertone, during the singing; but Ingibjorg paid no attention to her, keeping her eye fixed on Swerker, and endeavoured to attract his notice. It was in vain; he did not turn his face towards the nave.

'They are going to install him; look!' whispered the lady, touching Ingibjorg, as Swerker was conducted to the abbatial chair, the pastoral staff placed in his hands by one priest; the mitre of white silk, like a Scotch cap put on sideways, and bearing little

* Heimskringla Saga, xiii. 12.

resemblance to the present shape, was put over his white locks by another; then there was a general stir among the congregation.

'What is going to be done now?' asked Ingibjorg nervously; 'not going, are we, yet?'

'No, no,' whispered Gudruna's sister; 'we are all going to salute him; follow me. You must kiss his hand.'

Ingibjorg jumped up with precipitation. There was now a press of people into the choir, hurrying to greet the reverend man, and the two women were soon involved in the throng and had to follow the stream.

'You men!' exclaimed the lady; 'it is not polite to push me about,' and at the same time she herself was elbowing her way in the most determined manner.

'Now then,' she ejaculated, as she got through the choir door in the screen, and her towering head-dress struck the beam and nearly fell off. 'Here, Ingibjorg, help this cap right; it is dropping from my head.'

Her hair fell from beneath it over her ear, and she was compelled to stand aside beyond the crowd to readjust the tiara. Ingibjorg cast back a look of defiance at the lady and pushed on with the rest. In another moment she was before the abbot, had thrown herself on her knees and clasped his hands.

'What dost thou want, daughter?' asked the good old man, looking into her imploring face.

'Save me, save me!' she cried. 'I have been

dragged away from home and cannot get back without your help.'

Swerker keenly examined her features. 'I have seen you before,' he said. 'Do you not come from Oræfa-dal?'

'I do, I do indeed!' Ingibjorg exclaimed, still holding his hand firmly. 'You must help me get back to my parents; they know not what has become of me.'

'How has all this come to pass?' asked the abbot, with considerable surprise.

'Father,' said Gudruna's sister, stepping up, with some agitation of voice, 'you must not listen to this pert and foolish girl, I beg you; she is my servant.'

'Daughter,' exclaimed the priest sternly, 'this maiden is no servant, but the daughter of an honourable bonder. Whether you have been the cause of her being carried from home, I do not know; enough that you have no right to keep her. I take her in charge myself.'

'I was carried off by force,' sobbed the girl. 'My servant was killed, and here am I sent to be a woman's slave, whilst my poor father and brothers are in alarm for my sake, not knowing where to seek me.'

'Fear not, daughter,' said the abbot kindly. 'You shall be sent home as soon as possible.'

'That shall she not,' exclaimed the lady, with a loud, firm voice. 'My slave she is and shall be; I shall summon thee, proud priest, for this before a Thing. She shall come with me. Ingibjorg, come with me instantly!'

The woman caught the girl by the arm with a powerful grasp to drag her away; and Ingibjorg, frightened and vacillating, scarcely knew how to resist, but 'Stop, daughter; I bid you stop!' exclaimed Swerker, laying his crozier between the two. 'This maiden is in the hands of the Church: I warn thee, beware how thou meddlest with her.'

'I care not,' cried the lady, dashing the pastoral staff aside.

Ingibjorg sprang from her grasp and took refuge beside the abbatial throne on her knees, holding firmly to the arms of the seat.

Several of the bystanders now interposed. Some were for removing Gudruna's sister; others, her connections or friends, took her side, and the choir was likely soon to become the scene of a general uproar, when the corkscrew head-dress, which had been waving above all heads, either came in contact with the flame of one of the candles; or the wick, which the acolyte had neglected to snuff, fell on it, and in a moment the gauze erection was in flames. There was a rush, the head-dress was torn off and trampled under foot, a scuffle ensued and an outcry of fire, and the lady only regained perfect consciousness when she found herself beyond the door, surrounded by anxious friends, and quite uninjured; but with her long black hair falling loosely about her face and shoulders, somewhat frizzled with the flames.

As soon as the service was over, the abbot was reconducted to the monastic buildings, and Ingibjorg, under the charge of the monk who kept the guest-house, was put in safety, and consoled with the assurance that she would be given an escort on the following morning, which would undertake to restore her to her father in the south of the island.

Ingibjorg was, however, destined to be released earlier than she expected; for shortly before dusk the porter of the monastery was brought to the gates by the sound of heavy blows, and a blast on the cowhorn suspended at the side.

On opening, he saw Thorarin and his companions standing without, and inquiring for the abbot.

The delight of the good old man at seeing them need not be described, nor his readiness to give them all the hospitality the monastery could afford. Ingibjorg was brought to her brother and fell sobbing into his arms.

'Father,' said Thorarin, after a short consideration, ' will you let us have horses that we may ride towards home this night? My father will be filled with deepest anxiety till he knows the end of my expedition; if I ride to-night I may reach the Lomagnupr by morning, cross the Firth at daybreak, and be at Oræfa-dal to-morrow. Besides, we are more likely to escape observation if we depart at once. The lady Steinvor has many relations and friends, and they may oppose us. Not that I fear; but having a sister with me, I must use some precaution.'

Swerker pondered a moment; at last he took Thorarin's hand, saying, ' My son ! it shall be as you wish. I believe that you are in the right; the Hraunvellir family are dangerous to deal with. I

knew one '—his brow saddened and he heaved a low
sigh—' Tu homo unanimis, et notus meus : qui simul
mecum dulces capiebas cibos : in domo Dei ambula-
vimus cum consensu.'

As he murmured lowly to himself, he opened the
door and led Thorarin and Ingibjorg forth. A monk
stood without, and as he heard the old man's last
words, he added the next verse of the Psalm, ' Veniat
mors super illos,' but Swerker started, and shook
his head. ' Far be it from that,' he said.

The bell began slowly to toll for evening service.
' My children,' said the abbot, ' in another hour all
will be ready for your journey; you can leave the
horses at the ferry, and they shall be sent for to-
morrow. I am going to the church now; Heaven
bless you both.'

The choir alone was lighted that evening, and
only dimly did the feeble flare of the lamps smite
against the black roof. Tall, shadowy, the great
cross over the screen threw a long shade down the
empty nave. The voices, unaccompanied by the
Langspiel, rose and fell in unison as they sang the
Psalms. Swerker's mind reverted involuntarily to
Eric in the choir of Skalholt, to his loss, his falling
away; and the old man's heart was filled with
sorrow, harmonizing with the plaintive sweetness
of the chant. The venerable man's heart seemed
to him that night strangely filled with the poor
prodigal.

' I cannot think how it is,' murmured the old man
to himself, as he walked across the quadrangle to
the guest-house after the conclusion of the evening

service, ' I cannot think how it is that poor Eric should thus weigh down my thoughts this night.'

Thorarin, his sister, Alf, and Einar rode from the gate, and the abbot stood in the door with bare head looking after them. The soft twilight of an autumn night filled the sky, a tender light still flushed the glacier heads of the Skaptá and distant Oræfa Jökulls, but their bases were lost in a swimming gray. The cold wind fluttered the old priest's white hair and the skirts of his cassock, as he lingered on the threshold, looking far away with moistened eye, and his lips murmured again and again, ' Oh, Eric, my son, my son !'

High overhead a skua gull flew, and the light smote on his white wings against a dusky sky. One sharp note rang from the abbey bell ; a wheeling bat had struck it in its flight. Far off the waves plashed with a heavy fall on the shingle beach, the tide was rising. There was a kindling in the sky, and long rays of soft, rosy light streamed across it—a gush of pink in the north, brightening as the shadows of the hills fell deeper about their roots, and all little things in the vales lost themselves in the rising gloom ; it was the Aurora Borealis.

The old abbot quietly stepped within the gates, closed them after him with a sigh, and with his sigh still whispered, ' Oh, my son, my son !'

CHAPTER XXII.

CONFLICT.

HORARIN and his sister rode at a quick trot over the sandy ground, followed at no very great distance by the two servants. Ingibjorg related to her brother the events which had taken place as far as she was aware of them, and she knew more about them than either he or his father.

After some hesitation she even told him of her affection for Eric, of his having escaped from confinement through her instrumentality, of the means employed by Thorstein the Fox to induce her to come beyond the farm precincts with him.

She was well aware that she had been confided to the tutelage of Eric's aunt, the lady Steinvor, but whether her lover were privy to it or not she could not tell. Thorarin, on the other hand, related his adventure in Hraunvellir Farm; the strange conduct

of Eric in that case was a mystery which he and his
sister were together unable to unravel.   Time passed
rapidly, and the cavalcade had advanced quickly
while engaged in conversation.   The road now
dipped into a long glen between bare scarps of tufa
and iron-gray lava.

The Aurora had been rapidly brightening, and
Ingibjorg called her brother's attention to it.   They
drew up their horses to look at the heavens.   ' I
never saw the northern light so very brilliant in
Norway as it is here and on this evening, did you,
Thorarin ?' asked Ingibjorg.

Suddenly a rattle and roll under ground, so loud
as to alarm the horses, passed up the glen and
moved west.   It seemed as if the cliffs swayed, and
the ground rose and then fell ; large fragments broke
off from the sides of the valley, and fell splintering
and crashing down the shady slopes.   At the same
time, a furious blast of wind drove up the ravine,
beat in their faces, and then they heard it roaring
through the whortle and heather shrubs of the plain
from which they had descended.   The echoes from
the concussion of falling blocks had hardly died
away when a spear suddenly whirled through the
air, struck the saddlecloth, entered the shoulder of
Thorarin's horse, and brought it snorting to the
ground.   Before he could extricate himself, three
men sprang upon him.   Ingibjorg shrieked with
terror, and the two servants galloped up.   Alf
brought his sword down on the man who was
nearest his master; the wounded horse plunged up
and fell again, so that Thorarin was enabled to

disengage himself and draw Magnus' great sword from his back, and with a shout of rage to rush upon his assailants.

'As I live!' shouted Alf, 'Thorstein the Fox!'

'Right,' answered the fellow, with a laugh.

'I owe you a reckoning!' exclaimed Alf, urging his horse upon him.

Thorstein knelt to elude the meditated blow, and drove his sword into the horse's heart.

'Sister,' called Thorarin after Ingibjorg, 'ride on!' The girl had caught sight of her lover among the assailants, and plaintively and despairingly she cried, 'Brother, do not hurt Eric!'

In another moment Thorarin and the sub-deacon were engaged.

The broad blue sword Thorarin had borrowed from Magnus stood him in good stead. Eric was armed with a shorter weapon, and with a circular shield covered with leather, which he wheeled skilfully about on his left arm, warding the blows of the ponderous sword of his adversary.

Thorstein's natural impetuosity was somewhat restrained by the size of his weapon, which could be used only with precaution and tardily, being wielded with two hands. Eric, on the other hand, headstrong and blinded with his fury, sought to escape the sweeps of the two-edged blade, and get to close quarters, where his own weapon would be useful. Thorarin backed from his reach, was collected, though full of fire. At one moment he retreated, at another had leaped a lava-block, and Fireheart was whirled from another quarter. Thorarin fought, in fact,

13

with hearty goodwill; occasionally he would run from his antagonist and deal a blow in behalf of Alf or Einar, then, returning with a shout, face the furious sub-deacon. One of these strokes had wounded Thorstein the Fox so severely that the fellow had left the sorely-oppressed Alf, and betaken himself to safety among the rocks. Einar was slightly wounded, but kept his ground against two, till Alf, being released from Thorstein, was able to assist him.

In the meantime Fireheart had with one blow doubled and rent Eric's shield. The sub-deacon with a furious oath flung it aside, seized his sword with two hands and rushed upon his enemy. Thorarin saw his advantage, lifted Fireheart in readiness, and stepped back precipitately. The Aurora flamed crimson overhead and flashed back red from the swords.

Down came Thorarin's weapon, sweeping Eric's sword aside with one mighty blow; then checked sharply, with a bold back-handed stroke smote the sub-deacon in the side. Eric frantically lifted his weapon and leaped like a cat towards his foe. But Thorarin, satisfied that his stroke had sufficed, sprang from his place, and rejoined Alf and Einar. Eric attempted to pursue him, but his legs tottered, he supported himself for a few minutes on his sword, and then fell on the sand.

All conflict was now at an end, and Thorarin stood beside his wounded foe with a sorrowful face. Eric's angry eye flared back at him a dogged defiance.

'I have slain you,' said Thorarin. 'Right sorry for it am I, but that stroke is thy death-wound. Fain would I have only wounded thee a little.'

'And with Fireheart, too,' moaned the sub-deacon, beating his eyes with his palms; then removing them, he looked at his blood which trickled down the beautiful sword.

Thorarin stared at him with astonishment.

'What dost thou mean by Fireheart? Tell me if there be anything I can do for thee, any message I can take for thee—yes, even into the den of that tigress thy mother, where I could fight my way to deliver it—that would be all the pleasanter!'

Eric writhed on the ground; he looked up into his victor's face and said:

'Yes, tell her that I am killed, cut down by old Fireheart; tell her that, and bid her avenge me.'

Then he dropped his face into the black sand, spurning and tearing at the pebbles and dust in impotent rage.

'I will readily take that message,' observed Thorarin. 'But, friend, I should like to know what you mean by Fireheart. I would, too, that you were calmer and more ready to die like a Christian, if die you must. Here, give me your hand.'

Eric pressed his palm against his side.

'Fireheart, poor sword, poor sword!' he moaned.

'What know you of this sword? Why do you call it Fireheart?' asked Thorarin, wiping the perspiration from his brow.

Eric lifted himself on his elbow, looked fiercely at him, and said:

'How do I know Fireheart, my father's sword?
How do I know you to be my father's murderer?
Ah! do you ask me that?'

'Your father's sword!' echoed Thorarin, in
astonishment. 'My friend, you are in some grievous
error.'

'I am not,' shouted Eric, in a wild, hard tone.
'I know it well enough, and that you have murdered
my father in Norway to get it.'

'Heaven forbid!" exclaimed Thorarin. 'My
brother got this weapon from a man who was killed
by wolves; it was on the occasion when he saved
little Asmund.'

'Asmund!' said Eric, in a failing voice; 'Asmund
was killed, too—he was my brother.'

Thorarin looked hard into the face of the sub-
deacon, and saw that life was ebbing. 'I will swear
to you, friend,' he said quietly—'I swear to you
that we came by this sword in no unlawful way;
that my brother's head and mine are clear from
your father's blood. How these matters have come
about I cannot understand, and you cannot bear to
search it out now.'

Eric's eyes rested on Thorarin's countenance
steadily; at last he sighed heavily, and muttered, 'I
believe you, I believe—carry me to Kirkjubæ.' In a
few moments he had fainted away.

Thorarin bound up the sub-deacon's wound to
the best of his power, lifted him on Einar's horse,
and supported him in his seat while Alf led the
animal. Ingibjorg had come back, and she rode
sobbing in the rear.

The skies burned with a ruddier glow of crimson, the light being clearer over the Oræfa, whose crest was covered with thick mist, and filming gradually towards the west. All the mountain-tops except the Oræfa were free from fog.

The wind blew cool in the wounded man's face and revived him. Thorarin gave him water to drink, and the horse ambled along. The great voice of the sea was audible from the plain as the waves swept the cliffs, for the tide was at its height, just turning. The fire overhead throbbed in pulsations of pink light, and at one moment broke into flakes of flame. Another earthquake shock, but not so loud as the former, clashed below; and shortly after the roar and shiver of a huge line of wave was borne down on the ear by the breeze. Gulls seemed strangely alert at that hour; numbers flew west, their discordant screams sounding strangely fearful from the fire-dappled sky. Shortly after the mists off the Oræfa were carried along by the wind, and, ascending the glens from the Lomagnupr, spread over the tableland which the party were crossing, and enveloped them in a hot, steaming fog, having a pungent smell. It lasted for a short while only, and then blew off. Kirkjubæ church and monastery now stood out darkly against the horizon.

Eric had been growing feebler and fainter, and now he drooped over Thorarin's arm. Just before they came to the gates he sank from the horse and lay fainting on the turf. Ingibjorg herself brought water and poured it over his pale face, and when his languid eyes opened they rested mournfully on hers.

'Ingibjorg!' he whispered softly, and felt with his hand; she took it between her own.

Einar sounded the horn at the gate.

Thorarin supported Eric's head. No one spoke, for all waited till Swerker the abbot should come.

The monastery door opened, and the lights glimmered through the gate on the wet grass. The porter brought the abbot to the wounded man, and when Eric saw the old man's face he closed his heavy eyes and trembled. Swerker took his hand and pressed it; he seemed to divine all by the girl's sobs, and he said softly to her:

'My child, you must be prepared for the worst. And yet I do not despair. We have a very famous leech in the monastery, who knows the properties of herbs.'

The prodigal looked earnestly from Thorarin's breast, and the glaring sky seemed fearfully to irradiate his countenance.

'Blood—all is blood,' he muttered between his teeth.

'Not so,' said the abbot; 'light—all is light.'

He summoned a couple of monks.

'Bear this man to the infirmary,' said he. 'Bear him gently, for he is in pain. I am not wise in these matters. I have, thank heaven! not been engaged in deeds of violence. I see he has been wounded, but I do not believe that his condition is hopeless, though he be in danger. A quiet mind, patience, and trust will do him great good. Where is Brother Rognvald?'

'He has hastened to stew down some herbs of which he knows the virtues,' answered a monk.

'That is well,' said the abbot; 'Rognvald is our great leech. He has learned much in England.'

Then the wounded man was gently raised and carried with the utmost precaution to the infirmary, followed by Thorarin and his sister.

'I have been wondering,' said the abbot. 'I must send for his aunt, the lady Steinvor. I deem it wise for you now to leave the unfortunate young man in our hands and hers. You ride away to Oræfa-dal, and trust that we will do our utmost to restore the unhappy Eric, not in body only, but in mind as well. You have your father to consider. If you start late, by that time Steinvor of Laug will have heard that you have wounded her nephew. She is of a nature almost as violent as that of Eric's mother. She will summon all her servants, send round to all her relatives, and fall upon you. She is not one to listen to argument, to wait for explanations. Therefore, I say, make haste and depart. You have been involved in one fray already that has had a serious end; avoid the chance of another.' Then the old man conducted Thorarin and Ingibjorg to the gate; the servants were waiting for them, the horses ready.

Again the abbot was about to dismiss them, when there was a sudden flare in the east; all turned with a start, and saw a globe of lurid flame shoot up from the Oræfa crest, followed by a roar and shiver in the ground. A dense column of black cloud in another instant enveloped the mountain-top.

'Good heavens!' gasped the abbot, his face paling with fear—'the Oræfa!'

CHAPTER XXIII.

AN ERUPTION.

MUCH about the time that Thorarin was conducting his wounded foe to the monastery, traversing the high table-land by Kirkjubæ, another party was crossing the spur of the Oræfa which ran towards Hòf; for Gudruna, impatient of ever getting her son's assistance, had assembled and armed a band of farm-servants, and was conducting them by night to surprise and burn Gregorius in his farm.

As the mountain-crest was reached, all paused.

To the south-west the sea glittered in the moon, or
flashed back the fire of the Aurora; one little
fishing-boat lay as a black speck in the pathway of
pure silver traced on the ocean, and then, speeding
on, its white sails caught the gleam in the water
beyond. There was a red flame on deck from the
torches held by the fishers to lure the herring,
and, as the moon lost the sail, the place of the little
barque would have been lost too, but for the ruddy
star.

In the hush of night, the wavelets playing on the
pebbles in the Lomagnupr frith could be heard by
those far up the mountain-side. North-east the
vapours hung about the Oræfa in dense piles, at
one moment rising into spires, kindled by the fire
overhead, at another swept off by the wind into a
long trail of white flying fog which was drifted over
the estuary to the highlands beyond.

' We shall soon be at Oræfa-dal !' exclaimed Olver,
as he pointed down the valley which lay in deep
shadow at their feet.

' Stand close for a few moments first,' said
Wielund ; ' we shall be enveloped in mist directly ;'
and in another moment an arm of the vapours about
the Oræfa crest rolled up the valley and surrounded
them. It was rather steam than mist, and smelt
strongly of sulphur, so strongly as to make the men
cough.

' I never was in a fog like this before,' observed
Wielund, as the wind caught it and carried it out to
sea. ' It is my opinion that something uncommon
is about to take place. I have been watching the

birds to-day, and they have been flying from
this part of the country. Then, we have felt a
good many earthquake shocks of late, two this evening, and one of these was as violent as any I can
remember.'

'If you recollect, Wielund,' said Olver, 'the Oræfa
river was amazingly swollen, and there have not been
rains enough to account for it.'

'Press on!' exclaimed Gudruna; 'if we remain
chattering on the hill-top, day will dawn and the
rats escape.'

'Look, look at the sea!' cried one of the men.

As far as they could see was a long ridge of wave
bowling towards shore; it burst on the beach with a
heavy roar, and the coast-line appeared marked
with foaming and fretting water.   In another
moment the tide dropped as rapidly, leaving sands
uncovered which had never before been seen, and
then it swept in again and rose to its former level.
Wielund shook his head and began to descend.
The others followed, stepping cautiously among the
blocks of tufa and patches of snow.   Gudruna felt
her way with the dagger; her eyes turned frequently
with savage satisfaction to the blood-red sky, which
lit the snowy mountains and broad shoulders of
glacier with a lurid glare, where they were not fog-
wrapped.   The party entered a ravine which wound
between high scarps of lava towards the roots of the
mountain.

The darkness in this cleft was considerable enough
to enhance the difficulty of advancing, and all were
compelled to proceed with great caution.   A large

snowy owl was on the alert, dashing from side to
side of the gorge uttering discordant whoops; whilst
the pretty snow buntings, instead of being at roost,
were fluttering upon the ground, or fleeting through
the darkness with timid chirps, bewildered with
fear.

'Stop!' cried Wielund authoritatively.

All halted, and there ran a chill through the
stoutest heart as they felt the ground rock and sway
beneath their feet. There was a crash—then a shrill
whistle which broke into roarings like a bull. At no
great distance in the rear all saw a column of steam
burst from a rift in the lava-rock; at first it shot
upwards as a long, thin jet, but the crag on each
side was soon splintered with the heat, and the
bellowing of the mighty blast was reverberated in
thunder from the cliffs on both sides. The wind
drove the steam down the ravine, and all but
suffocated the party. In a moment their clothes
were drenched, and their hair and beards beaded
with drops. They ran and stumbled in haste to
escape from the hot fumes, and at length stood freed
from the steam at the mouth of the chasm. A cry
of astonishment escaped their lips.

Below, the Oræfa valley was half filled with a
rolling mass of turbulent water, like blood, as it re-
flected the Aurora-kindled heavens. It was a huge
driving flood, dancing blocks of ice on its surface, and
drifting great boulders up the banks.

'Where is the farm?' asked Gudruna.

'Where?' echoed Olver. 'Heaven knows whether
we shall return; this is not all.'

'It is *not*,' said Wielund ; and as he spoke, a flake of vivid fire, so bright as to kindle the whole prospect and light up their fear-blanched countenances, broke from the summit of the Oræfa, rose to the zenith, and burst over the whole sky into myriads of lambent blue flames. Then a shock and roar, a bowing together of the earth in pangs, a grinding and rending ; all were thrown on their faces, and when they looked again a cloud of black was rising from the Oræfa, through which lightnings played and flames flickered and danced. It spread above as a wide unfolding canopy, blotting out the Aurora, the wan stars, the calm moon, extinguishing all light, till the horizon itself was lost, and a curtain of utter darkness wrapped everything in one frightful pall, rent at intervals by red streaks of fire in the north-west, and by blinding flashes overhead. A thin, almost impalpable sand began to fall, and now and then red-hot ashes struck the earth and lighted the soil for an inch around. No one spoke—they could not have been heard had they attempted, for the concussions of falling crags, the bellowing of the mountain, the rumble of thunder, along with the grating of the driven rocks in the flood, deafened and stunned. Something rubbed the men's legs, and they could hear faint bleatings at their feet— some scared sheep had found refuge on the same spot ; a large bird dropped, beating its wings against Wielund's face — no one could see what bird it was. The darkness deepened as the black dust fell thicker; utter was the gloom before, but now even the fire from the mountain crest could not be seen, and the lightnings cast but a blear gleam. There was a sharp crack, a streak of flame in front of their eyes ; they could see one of their comrades struck *into* the sand, doubled, and beaten down by a large fragment of stone half molten—they could see alone by the light of the vitrified block itself.

Then there fell a stillness over all ; the first pangs of the volcano were passed, and the roarings momentarily were hushed; all that was audible was the grinding of the ice in the river, and the roll of the waves, and *that* they seemed to hear through their feet, the air was so thick with sand ; they could hear, too, the snapping and crackling of the fiery block which had smitten down their companion, as it slowly cooled.

'Lady Gudruna,' said Wielund, in a low, faltering voice, ' art thou near ?'

He was answered by a sob.

'Fear not, lady, we shall——'

'Fear !' cried Gudruna's voice shrilly through the darkness; 'I only fear that I shall not have my revenge;' she sobbed again, then moaned, 'Oh, Eric, Eric! we shall die here, and your father will remain unrevenged. Eric, Eric! Come on,' cried Gudruna, 'come on, friends.' She paused. 'Are you all coming?' she asked, for nothing could be seen.

'We are,' answered some voices.

The way was mostly even, lying on slopes of sand, but occasionally masses of stone struck the feet, and the lady and her attendants had carefully to pick their way by feeling.

Neither Gudruna nor any of her companions spoke. They had lost all knowledge of the direction in which it had been their purpose to go. As they were thus standing in uncertainty, they heard the weeping of a child hard by, and then a man's voice saying :

' Have no fear, little Asmund ; kneel and pray ; then the good God will have care for thee.'

Gudruna trembled—it was as though her dead husband spoke to her dead little one in Paradise— and she heard the voice, but saw no man.

' " Our Father, which art in heaven," ' was said in a child's clear tones. Gudruna knew these notes : they were those of her own lost Asmund. A great fear crept over her heart.

There ensued another earthquake shock, accompanied by the roarings of the mountain and the gleam of lightning overhead. The river lashed and boiled below : they were on a crag above the water ; and as a huge stone was dashed against it, the rock shook with the concussion.

Hour after hour passed, and the darkness remained unabated ; all sat down in the places where they had been standing, and awaited death. Rocks snapped and tottered on all sides, huge stones whizzed past, bounding from cliffs on the mountain scarp above, and plunged into the boiling river ; large splashes of rain fell, not in thin drops, but in hot, heavy gouts ; the air was impregnated with sulphur which had acidulated the rain, and began to condense on the hair and eyelashes. Those exposed had their mouths, ears, and eyes filled with black dust, which pained and irritated almost insupportably. It was impossible to tell whether day had dawned, for the dark smoke canopy utterly withheld the feeblest glimmer from reaching them.

At one moment, however, there was a change. The roaring of the mountain intensified, but was almost overborne by a new sound, one so frightful and deafening that its origin could not be conjectured. At once a gust of steam covered everything. Everyone flung himself with face to earth to escape the agonizing heat; the river poured up the rock, and some of its warm spray swept over it. The clash and jar at its sides seemed enough to rip it up and whirl it along in the eddies of the torrent. Then the stream fell; the clouds of steam condensed, and left a vacuum below—for a few moments. The terrified men looked over the ledge of rock. The river was almost dried up, but up the valley they saw spread out a mass of fire, pouring from the mountain roots, and filling the torrent bed. By its white glare the lower portion of the valley could be seen ; great blocks of ice lay stranded high up the sides, and were melting rapidly into little streams which trickled down to the fiery flood, and then lost themselves in puffs of steam. Water-sodden carcases of cows and horses strewed the margin ; one large beast had been jammed between two boulders, and faced erect the slowly-advancing lava. Shattered roofs and timber gate-posts lay here and there, and were consumed instantaneously by the river of flame. Not a trace of field or inclosure could be made out ;

the Oræfa torrent had rent the whole valley into
long parallel rifts and wounds, heaping up in places
piles of rubble, crowned by tottering masses of stone.
The earthquake had at one point torn a deep chasm
across the bed of the stream; this had remained full
of water when the lava had cut off the river, but now
the fused matter roared down the rent, converting
the water into steam, which blew off in whirling
pillars.   In another moment, the cloud of black
dust fell again, the light from the lava was extin-
guished, and no man could see the hand he held
before his face.

Hour after hour passed; the sounds continued
with the same stunning reports; lightning flared,
and thunder crashed almost without intermission.
Most of the men lay with their faces in their arms in
mute despair; Gudruna wrapped her dagger to her
bosom and rested her head upon her knees.   During
pauses in the discharges and detonations, a child's
whimpering could be heard close by, and sometimes
a manly voice comforting the little one; but no
words could be distinguished.

Hour after hour of the blackness of the grave
without its rest.   Hour after hour of the despair and
horror of outer darkness surrounding the living.
Sometimes a man would extend his arm and grope
for a handful of snow or a fragment of ice, to wash
the sand from his eyes and cool his tongue.   Sometimes one would pull up a tuft of grass, and hope to
stop his ears to the sounds, only to find that every
nerve was endowed with hearing, and that those
fearful noises could not be shut out; then he would

wrap his head again in his cloak with a groan. Sometimes a horror would fall upon one man, and he would think himself alone—then he would cry as with pain, but all were too indifferent to answer him; he would crawl shivering along till he felt the arm of a comrade, and even then be unsatisfied till he had made that one move to certify that he was living also. Sometimes a sort of famine for rest would come over another, and he would creep to the verge of the precipice, that he might cast himself down in hopes of quiet in death, anything being, he thought, better than the blackness and the din which surrounded and bewildered him; but then, when he felt himself at the edge, and found that there was no standing ground in front, it seemed too ghastly a thing to fall—he knew not whither—perhaps to some bubbling pit of hot mud, perhaps into some vast rent and abyss, which went down to the fire in the earth's womb; he would recoil and clamber away on hands and knees, his hair bristling with terror lest accidentally he *might* fall.

Sometimes a man would strive to collect his thoughts and pray, but his thoughts could not be collected, and pray he could not—he might only tremble; so then a new agony of horror would curdle through his marrow, for he thought he must be in hell itself, where prayer is impossible. Then, too, he knew not where his life had ended and death had begun, how he had slipped so easily from one into the other; he fancied that his comrades lay like sheep in the outer darkness with him; and that wailing child which he saw not, only heard—that

14

was in torment too. The black sand heaped about
them ; if they kept their hands in one place, soon
they were covered, and soon would be buried in
dust ; and the rock could scarce be felt, save when
one scraped through a hand's depth of soft powder.

There was a shriek ! One man had thought that
this was never to end—this was hell for ever and
ever. He shrieked at that bare thought and fainted
away. No one else moved. Gudruna gnawed her
mantle till she gnawed it through, and the sand
came between her lips. Olver lay on his face, and
the dust rose about him ; he would not rise, he let it
be so—die so as well as any other way; and a red
fallen cinder lay on the lappet of his dress, which
smouldered away like a bit of tinder; he let it be so
—nothing mattered any longer. One man, his teeth
set, his knuckles pressed hard into his eye-sockets,
filled up his black heart with hate for his enemies,
and hope that they, too, might be in the same con-
demnation.

There was a slight clearing in the darkness, a
cooler air on the cheek, and then, of a sudden, one
wondrous change. Some looked up suddenly to see
Paradise unclosed to them in vain. There was an
instantaneous rending of the black veil by a fresh
sea gale. Right and left the heavy, lumbering clouds
of sooty tinge were beaten, as a way of clear, pure
air opened in the valley.

All saw a wondrous sight. The clouds as dark
drapery extended on each side to the zenith, leading
up to the Oræfa, at whose head and base glared the
lava streams. The sun was out, and lit the large

rounded domes of snowy fog which stood high above
the black cloud against fair depths of blue. A long
belt of gold fell over the rent and shattered valley,
its coppice woods turned to a dull gray, its emerald
turf swept away to sea. In that celestial beam the
lava whitened and hid its flare. South lay the
Breidamark Bay, whimpling with blue, and sparkles
on its curling waves over the sand-bar. Wondrous
seemed that beauteous sky, paling tenderly to the
sea horizon, to eyes which for many hours had been
blinded by night. The shadows of the clouds
dappled the sea with green, but within the bar
the water was blue as heaven itself, calm and wave-
less, and on it floated the *Puffin* and the *Dragon*.

Sweet with the fragrance of sea-weed was the
breeze which played up the valley, and cooled the
fagged and jaded faces of those assembled on the rock.

They looked at each other and about them.
Gudruna sprang to her feet. Close by, on the same
shoulder of rock, sat Gregorius with little Asmund
in his arms, and Magnus knelt by his side, gazing
eagerly at the sea. The bonder stroked the dust
from Asmund's cheek, and said : ' Magnus, bring me
a little snow; the child is hurt and ill.'

Gudruna stepped forward with throbbing breast
till she stood opposite, looking intently on the little
boy's face; it was soiled, and his fair hair clogged
with sand. She stooped and peered closely at him ;
the pure gold of the sun was on his thin countenance.

' Asmund!' exclaimed Gudruna, as the boy looked
listlessly at her through his blue eyes. ' Asmund!
you are my son!'

CHAPTER XXIV.

CONCLUSION.

GUDRUNA
&
ASMUND

GREGORIUS seemed scarcely to understand the exclamation of Gudruna, for his mind was intent on the murky coils of cloud which towered from the Oræfa.

'A signal from the *Puffin!*' cried Magnus, as a red streamer danced from the ship's mast. 'Glum is on board, father; let us hasten down to the shore.'

'Right!' exclaimed the bonder; 'nowhere is there safety except at sea. Lady! whoever you may be, and those with you'—he addressed himself to Gudruna—'in the bay lie my two boats; follow me and let us escape; this darkness may fall around us again, and all hopes of flight be cut off.'

As he spoke he began to descend, and all readily followed; but Gudruna grasped him by the shoulder, saying hastily, ' Give me my child ; let me carry him.'

Gregorius looked with surprise into her face, but the peril of delay was too urgent to allow him to question her. He said, therefore, ' Take the little boy, then, but bear him gently ; he has been sadly injured by some of the falling rafters of the house as we made our escape during the earthquake.'

Then he relinquished Asmund into her arms. She clasped him so tightly to her mother's breast that he uttered a cry of pain. She pressed her hot lips to his forehead and staggered with him down the hill, supported by Olver, or she would have fallen re- peatedly ; she had no eyes but for her recovered child.

The beach was at length gained, and Glum put off from the *Puffin* in a boat. Directly his eye fell on Gudruna he uttered a growl of dismay, and, drawing his master aside, whispered in his ear :

' She will kill Asmund ; she it is who lives at Hraunvellir, who sent her son to stab you—who has carried off Ingibjorg—who half murdered Thorarin and myself—she-wolf!'

' Let us get safely on board and put out to sea,' answered Gregorius, ' then all shall be cleared up. She is in no condition to injure us now.'

Glum shook his head and muttered :

' No one would believe me when I warned them what would come of living in this Iceland ; now all must know to their cost how true I am.'

' Tell me, Glum,' said Gregorius, ' what has become of our men ? Have you seen any of them?'

'Few are missing,' answered the pilot; 'the
majority are on board the *Puffin* now, but I have
sent two parties in search of you; they will be on
the return directly.'

'I wish Thorarin and Ingibjorg were here,' sighed
the bonder.

'Be advised by me,' observed Glum, 'and we
will run up to the Lomagnupr frith; it is a good
harbour, and we shall intercept Thorarin as he
returns.'

Gregorius acquiesced, and then ordered as many
as could into the boat. It pushed off, and, after
having taken them to the *Puffin*, returned for the rest.
When all were on board the anchor was weighed,
and the ship was rowed slowly out of the bay; it
passed the gap in the sand-bar and danced on the
green sea waves.

The Oræfa looked strangely awful; its roots were
rent and torn, fearful chasms yawned across the
hillsides, and a long flow of lava slowly crept down
the vale. The crest of the mountain was lost in
steam and black cloud, rent at intervals by lightnings; the smoke column rising to a vast height, at
times like burning copper, at others black as jet.
The wind had shifted to the west, so that although
the fall of black ash and dust was very considerable
to the east of the mountain, all the Lomagnupr
estuary was bathed in sunshine.

Gudruna crouched in the prow, looking on her
child; she was in this position when Gregorius
came up to her. She did not notice him; she was
wrapt in the consideration of the little boy lying on

her knees sleeping, his pale face, resting on his hand, blackened with volcanic dust, his cheeks smeared with the sand mingled with his tears.

'Lady,' said Gregorius, 'I would gladly have a word with you.'

Gudruna looked up sharply. Her savage eyes flashed scorn and hatred at him; but for the little one who slept on her lap she would have leaped upon him.

'Lady,' continued the bonder, unmoved by her glance, 'you called that boy your son; I would fain know what right he has to that title. He is none of mine, but an orphan whose parentage we have never known.'

'A lie!' snarled Gudruna through her teeth; 'you know well who he is; you know how he has become an orphan — because you have been his father's murderer.'

'God forbid!' exclaimed Gregorius, 'God forbid!'

Gudruna gazed with defiance into his eyes, as she said deliberately:

'You know that my husband Onund came to Norway to see you about the purchase of Oræfa-dal, and to place this little one as a foster-child with you; you know that you and he fell out about the price and that you killed him.'

'I did no such thing!' answered the bonder with indignation; 'whoever has told you such a tale is a liar! My son Magnus rescued this child from the wolves which slew the father. We never knew the name of the man whom the beasts killed, nor more of this little lad than that his name is Asmund. Ask the boy.'

Gudruna looked right and left in doubt and dismay. Her son woke with a sigh. She bowed her face over his, and said in a low voice, 'Asmund.'

'Yes,' answered he, looking up.

'Tell me, child, about your father. Do you remember him?'

The boy shuddered and hid his face with a moan.

'Tell me how he died,' she asked again.

'Oh, the wolves—those horrible wolves!' he cried with anguish, and half deliriously asked, 'Are they here too; are they coming on to tear me to pieces?' Then he buried his face in Gudruna's arm, trembling.

'Lady,' said Gregorius in turn, 'you must tell me how you came to hear that I had slain your husband. Someone has wickedly urged you on with a foul lie to cause my ruin.'

'I heard it from Hlenni, a Norwegian, in a letter,' answered Gudruna feebly. It began to dawn on her now that her vengeance had been poured on an innocent head, and her heart began to quake, for she knew that she had goaded on her eldest son to crime, and her youngest was dying in her lap.

'Hlenni,' said Gregorius, 'is my bitterest enemy. You should have inquired before believing such a report. Now, answer me: do you know where my daughter Ingibjorg is?'

'I do,' whispered Gudruna, for her voice failed her and her knees trembled; 'she is safe. I have given her into the care of my sister at Kirkjubæ.'

'Then Thorarin will have found her by this time!'

exclaimed the bonder joyfully. ' Eric went in pursuit of him, but what has happened to Eric I know not.' Gudruna sprang to her feet, and stood tottering and pale; her voice became shrill with anguish of soul.

'What have I done? I, his mother, urged him on to murder you in revenge for his father's death— you, who are innocent. When he loved your daughter, my blind rage could not bear the thought, and I had her carried away to Kirkjubæ. I sent him after your son to kill him, and now I know not what has befallen him, whether he has killed your son or been slain himself. Either way is evil! I came to burn you and your house, but the Oræfa had done that already.'

The *Puffin* rounded the promontory of Ingolf's-head and entered the fiord. A small boat which had been crossing, as soon as the vessel came in sight, altered its direction, and made towards it. By the time that the *Puffin* was anchored under one of the many sandy islets of the estuary, it had touched the vessel's side, and Thorarin and Ingibjorg, with their companions, had mounted the deck.

For a few moments father and daughter clung to each other speechless; then the old bonder removed his cap and knelt with folded hands on the prow, thanking God for the restoration of his child.

Gudruna stood immovable, her little boy wound in her arms and pressed to her bosom. Her eye caught Fireheart slung at Thorarin's back; but though her lips whitened with compression, not a word escaped. Asmund's eyes had been closed, and his breath had been coming shorter and shorter, while his cheek purpled at one instant and blanched at the next.

Gudruna could not cry, but only quiver with agony; not a moan or sigh relieved her. Then the little boy put up his hand, as if feeling for something; he touched her cheek, his eyes opened heavily, and a smile played on his lips; half unconsciously he stroked her face. The woman broke down and sank on the deck, her head buried in the child's face.

'Father,' said Thorarin, 'how is it that you have that fiend on board? I can guess why I find the *Puffin* here: you have escaped from the Oræfa.'

'Never mind how she comes here, son,' the bonder answered; 'you shall know that at another time; but tell me what you have done.'

'I have fought with and sorely wounded that woman's son,' said Thorarin, in a low voice. 'It was done in open fight, or rather in my own defence; and he has sent a message by me to his mother. He wishes me to tell her from him that the letter from Norway contained a lie.'

Gregorius bent his head.

'My son,' he remarked, 'we have been the object of hate and assault ever since we have been in Iceland, through the animosity of Hlenni. He charged us to this woman with the murder of her husband, little Asmund's father, and she has been ever since hungering and thirsting for revenge. God has shielded us, and turned her wrath against herself. You have wounded her eldest son, and Asmund has been so crushed by the falling timber of our roof that he will soon die. May God forgive her !'

' Hlenni again !' exclaimed Thorarin. ' I shall be off to Norway and punish him with my own hand.'

' Not so,' answered Gregorius. ' We need not bestir ourselves ; he is in the hand of One who will punish him in His own good time.'

Gudruna suddenly sprang to her feet, and held out the child in her arms. Asmund was already dead. Her face was calm and rigid and her voice firm as she spoke.

' Gregorius of Thordsa, listen to me. My child is taken from me at the hour that I recover him, and I am alone. I have wronged you, and all I ask is your forgiveness, for you shall never see me again. And that I may show you how truly I repent of the injuries I have unjustly done you, I call all present to witness that henceforth Hraunvellir shall belong to you should my son Eric die ; but should he live, then it shall belong to him and Ingibjorg. Forgive me.'

She bent one knee and touched Gregorius' outstretched hand ; then, rising, she beckoned to Olver, and stepped down into the boat, still clasping her dead Asmund to her heart. Her servant followed, and rowed her ashore. Gregorius and his children watched ; they saw her step out of the boat, sign to Olver that he should put back to the ship ; then they watched her climb the mountain-side ; they watched her toiling upward undauntedly, her child still to her heart. The black cloud of volcanic smoke rolled over the crest of the low ridge she was ascending. They could see her leave the last sun-gleam and climb in the shadow of that cloud; they looked still, and they saw her enter that darkness. No man ever saw her again!

THE END.

BILLING AND SONS, PRINTERS, GUILDFORD.

www.ingramcontent.com/pod-product-compliance
Lightning Source LLC
Chambersburg PA
CBHW030118030726
47498CB00007B/2448